ARTHUR

BOOK THREE, LOST VEGAS SERIES

LIZZY FORD

Published by Captured Press
www.CapturedPress.com

Cover design by Lizzy Ford
www.lizzyford.com

Arthur copyright © 2017 by Lizzy Ford
Cover design copyright © 2017 by Lizzy Ford

Published by Captured Press
ISBN-13: 978-1-62378-261-0

DEDICATION

For my furriends who keep me company while I write! Potato (bulldog), Tamale (shiba inu), Wookie (shih tzu), Tubbs (orange tabby), Curbie (mountain cur), and Poncho (Australian shepherd!)

CHAPTER ONE

ARTHUR'S SENSES AWOKE SLOWLY. First the crackle of a fire, then the heat against his left side contrasting against the cold chill numbing his exposed right cheek and hand. The comforting scent of burning wood was followed by an ache radiating throughout his body. He was sore, and the intensity of warm pain left him wondering if he had been thrown off a horse several times. The middle of his chest felt unusually hot, and he was not able to immediately assess whether he was injured there or not.

Unable to awaken fully, he slid again into the lingering vision, which played from the beginning once more.

Tiana wore the blue dress and bracelet he had envisioned in every iteration of the dream. Her blond curls bounced around her shoulders as she sprinted through a field and towards the sunrise, which had painted the sky pastel shades of pink and yellow. Unlike former versions of the possible future, this vision was different. Arthur saw more of her location. She ran away from a forest and towards the mountains, and four steps behind her, reaching out to grab her, was someone other than the skinwalker Arthur had envisioned every other time.

This time, their father, Edwin Hanover, chased Tiana.

Seeing the skinwalker in all his beastly forms pursuing Tiana had once terrified Arthur, but the expression on his father's face alarmed him more. Perhaps because he knew that look, and he understood what it meant to be on the receiving end of it. No one who incited his father's anger survived the day.

Arthur could not know, from this tiny glimpse, what had changed in their lives for this version of the future to materialize, but he did not doubt the message behind the vision.

Tiana remained in danger, except the skinwalker was no longer the greatest threat to her life.

The vision faded.

Arthur's senses gradually pulled him from semi-consciousness into the real world. As he became acquainted with his body once more, he sought some memory of why he was unconscious in the first place.

Tiana leaving his side ... the skinwalker walking into the middle of the village ... the black wolf's cold nose against his hand ... darkness.

Arthur's eyes snapped open. "Tiana," he breathed. His sister was alone, vulnerable, facing down a creature that had ripped through hundreds of lives in the short time Arthur had known him.

"Don't move!" Marshall Cruise's urgent whisper came from the other side of the fire.

Arthur froze. His senses picked up no danger, but his mind had not yet cleared of the fog left over from heavy sleep. What was the threat? The skinwalker? Natives? Ghouls?

Marshall knelt beside him and stretched towards the warm spot on Arthur's chest.

"What is it?" Arthur demanded quietly. "Am I badly wounded?"

Marshall snorted. "No. I was using you as an incubator."

Arthur's brow furrowed.

Marshall gently lifted a bundle off his chest, removing the source of pressure and heat. He leaned away and placed the bundle on the ground.

"Why?" Arthur asked.

"Another surprise from our magic wolf." Marshall

unwrapped the cloak.

Arthur sat up with a grimace. He had not been interrogated and beaten in two days, but he certainly felt as if he'd just left another round with Diving Eagle. "What …" His question faded as he peered over the edge of the bundle. His features softened into a smile. "How beautiful."

Several tiny puppies with eyes and ears not yet opened and pink stomachs slept in the bundle. Their coats ranged from white to gray to black, with one of them covered in brindle fur. They were small enough for two to fit in his hand, if he dared pick one up.

"Six," he counted. The number resonated within him, and his head shot up. "Where is the beast?" His heart began to race, and he stood.

"Not here," Marshall assured him. "The magic she-wolf whisked us away from danger."

"What do you mean?" Arthur noticed their surroundings for the first time. They remained in the forest – but no village or bonfires or people were visible in the night anywhere around them. Darkness fell outside the ring of light provided by the fire. His eyes went to the chains Marshall had pried off both of them and deposited at the edge of the firelight and settled on the wolf. "What happened to her?"

The she-wolf had turned whiter than starlight. She lay on the opposite side of the fire, unmoving, except for the steady rise and fall of her chest.

"You are more comfortable with this magic than I will ever be," Marshall replied curtly. "When I woke up, she was in labor, and we were all here. You were unconscious and would not respond when I tried to wake you. She was this strange shade of white. I helped her birth her babies, and she fell into a slumber from which she had not awakened. So I took her babies and wrapped them up to keep them warm."

Arthur went to the wolf and knelt beside her. Her breathing was steady and deep. She was alive with no labored breathing or twitching or any other sign her rest was imbued with discomfort.

He could not recall the last time he slept this deeply, and no wolf would survive past infancy if it slept in such a way it was unaware of the world. Though he did not feel connected to the wolf on an energy level, he could not help wondering if he were somehow.

"Even witnessing it, I cannot understand how we came to be here," Marshall said, unease in his tone. "And I do not know how far she took us."

"I can ask her when she wakes up."

"Oh, so she speaks to you? You forgot to mention that earlier."

Arthur was silent. He had explained, in as few words as possible, his gifts to Marshall while they sat in a cage in the Native warriors' village. He had also avoided speaking in too much detail of exactly what he could do, and had only provided general information. It was never wise to trust a Cruise with information that could send Arthur and his entire family to the stake.

No sooner did the thought cross his mind, than he recalled what news Tiana had brought him shortly before the skinwalker appeared.

Marshall's family was no longer a threat to anyone, here or anywhere. Arthur shifted the sleeping wolf closer to the fire and dug his hands into her thick fur, pensive. He had not wished to tell Marshall the truth about what the Hanover patriarch had done to the Cruises earlier, until they had escaped. Now that they were free, Arthur hesitated again.

They possessed one cloak between the two of them, which was being used to keep the wolf's puppies warm. Arthur saw no weapons or tools or anything he could use to hunt with, and even if they had something of that nature, neither he nor Marshall could spend more than an hour from the fire without freezing. They each wore a single, thin layer of clothing and boots.

He glanced at Marshall, who was carefully cradling the sleeping puppies. Guilt fluttered through him, along with an acknowledgment he and Marshall needed one another to survive the forest alone.

He could not reveal the truth now.

The silence between them weighed as heavy as his

conscience.

"I can speak to her," Arthur said. "Rather, she speaks to me. Usually in one or two word sentences, no more. I can sense danger as well, in a way unlike any skill a normal man possesses, and I have told you already of my visions of the future."

"You said you have few and they are as solid as dreams."

"That was not entirely true," Arthur admitted. "I cannot control when the visions come, but they are in great detail. My directional sense is not just for determining which cardinal direction we face, but can guide me anywhere I tell it to take me."

Marshall raised his eyebrows. "And you choose now to tell me this because why? You think we will die out here, and you feel the need to confess to your deformities?"

Confess, yes. "Take it how you will." Arthur did not like how it felt to lie to the man who saved his life more than once, and who chose to value the lives of the magical she-wolf and pups when he did not have to. If this kindness were not an indication of Marshall Cruise's nature, buried beneath his skepticism and resentful façade, then what was?

No matter what Arthur's father claimed about the Cruises, and how differently Marshall and Arthur saw the world, Marshall Cruise was a good man.

What other lies of my father's have I adopted without questioning? Arthur did not know this answer, which left him more troubled. Truth had little value to his father, or in their household, and he had never realized how skewed his perception of the world had to have been before this moment.

"What do you recall about the moment before we left?" he asked. "My sister was with us, and yet, she is not here."

"I heard someone shout and woke up in time to see you and the wolf vanish. All of the Natives were in the center of the village and your sister ..." Marshall drifted off. "Is she special, like you?"

Arthur did not respond.

"You lied about why we were hunting down that skinwalker in the first place, so I do not expect absolute honesty. I will, however, assume she possesses deformities of a different nature than yours," Marshall said shortly. "A commotion among the Natives awoke me. When I turned to talk to you, you were already gone. I saw Tiana lift the skinwalker into the air with magic and start to crush him."

It was Arthur's turn to be disbelieving. "Tiana?"

"Yes. That waif with the ghoulish eyes."

Arthur ignored the flush of heat inside him. It was hard to be angry with Marshall, even when he used such a disrespectful tone.

8

"She flung him against a tree and was crushing him when the wolf appeared out of nowhere and took me away," Marshall said. "I awoke here, beside you."

Arthur was silent. Tiana had never been permitted to allow her deformities to manifest. Their father forbade it, just as he secretly trained Arthur how to use his. Even so, Tiana trusted her brother more than anyone else and had revealed to Arthur a couple of her gifts. She used telekinesis to move her furniture and sometimes glimpsed the future, though not with the detail Arthur did, and she had admitted to crushing Matilda Cruise's head by accident when their stepmother tried to kill Aveline. It was *possible* she could lift a man.

But to lash out at a stranger? Some of the Native women had hit her, and Tiana did not complain or attack them. If she were going to hurt someone, self-defense was the rational time to do it.

"You are certain it was Tiana who did this and not some other deformed person?" Arthur asked, puzzled.

"I have never seen such an act in my life. It is stuck in my head." Marshall tapped his temple. "I know what I saw, Arthur."

"My sister has such deformities, but not the temperament. She would never hurt anyone for any reason," Arthur said.

"If she decided to make an exception, I am glad she chose to murder the skinwalker, or we would all likely be dead. As much as I despise pointless Hanover violence, I would also like to live to see my home again."

Arthur ignored the dig at his family, more interested in determining what motivated Tiana to act rashly. If he foresaw the skinwalker threat, had Tiana as well? He could not otherwise account for what she had done.

He rose.

Tiana, he ordered his magic silently. A faint breeze nudged him, and he faced the direction it indicated.

"Before you make some valiant claim that we need to save your sister, consider the fact we are stranded with a magic wolf and six puppies and little else in the middle of the forest," Marshall told him. "She is safer where she is than we are stranded out here among the Ghouls and wolves, assuming she destroyed the skinwalker as she appeared to be doing."

Without a vision proving Marshall right or wrong, Arthur did not feel nearly as comfortable making such an assumption. His sister had rarely been permitted outside her room and never left the city. She had no way of understanding the threats the Natives and forest posed to her or how to navigate them.

But ... he had seen her running from their father in the latest vision before he awoke. She was alive, though he was unable to guess in what shape.

"We need food and water," Marshall added. "I do not think you will want the wolf or her babies to die out here."

Arthur faced away from the direction in which Tiana was. "Of course not," he agreed. "She saved us again, and apparently, at great expense to herself."

"Then it is your turn to watch the pups while I sleep," Marshall said and stood from his place beside the fire. "They have eaten once and will probably be hungry again soon. I know I am." He approached and held out the bundle of pups. "This cloak is of spring quality, not winter. You will need to hold them to keep them warm."

Arthur accepted the bundle, once again disturbed by Marshall's compassion. Marshall did not coddle the animals but accepted the duty to care for them without question. Being good, *doing* good, was second nature to him.

No one in Arthur's family practiced or valued compassion, either.

Arthur watched the Cruise heir return to the far side of the fire and curl up on the ground, his back to the flames. Arthur sat and unfolded the cloak to peer at the tiny puppies again. Two white, one black, two gray, one brindle. They were piled atop one another, sleeping.

"I wonder if they are magic, too," he murmured.

"It they tell you, let me know," Marshall grumbled.

Arthur replaced the cloak and sat back, cradling the bundle as Marshall had. He shivered and moved closer to the fire. The early spring night was clear and crisp. His breath rose to the skies in visible clouds, and he mulled Marshall's claim about what happened before they were teleported way from the Natives' camp.

Why had the wolf saved them, if her master were in danger?

Why would she save them at all?

Too concerned about his sister to sleep, Arthur shifted the bundle of puppies to the side of the fire where their mother lay. If the wolf were ill, or did not wake up, he would face a difficult decision come morning. They needed to move, for fear of Ghouls or the Natives or hungry cats and wolves catching their scent, but would not go far if they were forced to carry the massive wolf.

Arthur waited until he heard the deep breathing and soft snores of Marshall before creeping closer to the wolf.

"Hey," he whispered and stroked her head. "Can you hear me?"

He stilled his hand and held his breath, waiting. No words emerged.

"I need to know if you are well enough to travel, or if you can heal yourself," he tried again. "I do not possess the healing magic. I know you do. You saved my life at the river."

Tingling, warm energy tickled his fingertips. She did not speak, but a faint vision entered his thoughts. It was too elusive for him to capture. Arthur closed his eyes to concentrate.

This time, he caught the quick, faded image of puppies in his mind.

He smiled. "They are all well and healthy," he reported. Withdrawing his hand, he picked up the bundle of sleeping pups and placed them on her side. "Maybe you can hear their hearts? Or feel their warmth?"

The fur beneath the bundle flushed black. The color blushed outward, darkening her unnatural white fur. The black circled the bundle and extended several inches out in each direction before it stopped.

Was this the magic of the wolves? A sign of some sort? Arthur had no way to explain her coat's return to its normal color in the area surrounding her babies. He rested his hand on her head once more and closed his eyes.

"All of us will be in danger if we remain here," he told her. "Of all the questions I want to ask you, only one needs to be answered now. If you have strength for more, we can talk for as long as you have the strength. But first, I must know, will you be well enough to travel soon?"

The image of a sunrise floated through his head before vanishing.

"Good," he said and released a sigh. His eyes went to Marshall, who slept soundly. Arthur had no intention of leaving his sister alone in the forest, even if what Marshall claimed was true. Arthur would rather hunt down a skinwalker and angry Natives than tell the man quickly becoming his friend what happened to his family.

CHAPTER TWO

ARTHUR DOZED OFF AND ON, too concerned about being exposed in the forest to sleep for long. When dawn crept through the clouds and past thick layers of branches, he roused himself fully. The bundle of pups in his arms was squirming. He shifted closer to the wolf and unwrapped them, setting the pups down close to their mother's belly. Despite their closed eyes, they sensed her and climbed over one another and the cloak to nurse.

He watched, smiling, then draped the cloak over the wolf and her babies to keep the morning chill from reaching them. The she-wolf remained silver-white, with the exception of the bloom of black from where he'd placed the pups on her side. He glanced at the wolf's face then back.

Her eyes were open. She didn't move, but she watched him.

"Good morning," he whispered. "Are you well enough to travel?"

Food.

Arthur sighed. "We have none and no weapons to kill game. We will find food today," he said firmly.

She did not respond, and he wondered if the self-sufficient wolf was irritated with humans who could not hunt for themselves.

Arthur stood with a grimace. His muscles were stiff. The cold morning carried a warm breeze, one he hoped meant the winter was finally ready to give way to spring. Shivering, he crossed to wake Marshall. The Cruise heir was trembling from cold in his sleep.

"Marshall, time to go!" Arthur said and shook his friend awake.

Marshall groaned. He stretched onto his stomach and then sighed loudly. "My stomach is eating itself!"

"Mine, too," Arthur said. "That is why we need to go …" He tilted his head and paused with a glance at the wolf.

The image in his mind was not the direction he had wanted. Not towards the city, not towards Tiana.

"North," he said.

"North?" Marshall asked and pushed himself onto his knees. "Is that not the opposite direction of anywhere we want to be?"

"It is." Arthur looked away from the she-wolf.

Marshall caught his glance and looked between the two. "Whose decision is this?" he asked.

"Hers."

"Why are we considering going north?"

Safe. Babies, she answered

"We cannot take her with us to the city," Arthur reasoned. "She cannot travel alone with her babes. We will situate her somewhere safe with her pups, then rescue Tiana and go home."

If Marshall doubted Arthur's plan, he did not show it. "We will need your father's army to rescue her. Our enemies will not free her willingly."

"If that is the case …" Arthur trailed off, unwilling to promise anything. Neither Marshall nor Tiana could return to Lost Vegas, or the Hanover leader would hurt them both. Arthur did not know how to protect his friend, especially when Marshall was ignorant of the danger. Traveling north would give him time to think.

Marshall shook his head. "If you had told me a month ago I would be at the mercy of a Hanover and a dog, I would have thought you madder than your father."

Arthur said nothing and hopped in place to keep warm.

The she-wolf had sat up, tugged off the cloak, and was grooming her babies. When they were clean and fed, the pups piled up next to her for warmth. Arthur collected them gently and replaced them in the cloak.

The wolf stood and shook off the leaves clinging to her fur. She gave the men a long look before turning and walking into the forest.

Arthur hastily kicked dirt over the embers of their fire. Marshall followed her, hugging himself and grumbling about the cold, lack of food, and the cursed Hanover's. Arthur trailed and listened to him with newfound patience – and a great deal of dread.

"Will we ever go home?" Marshall asked.

"Yes, we will," Arthur answered. It was inevitable that he would return to his home, and inevitable that Marshall discovered the truth. Of every thought on Arthur's mind, he could not help wondering if he had the power and influence necessary to save the remaining Cruise from his father. Marshall would hate Arthur for hiding the latest Hanover massacre, but this would not deter Arthur from protecting him.

Marshall grumbled more quietly this time.

Cold and miserable, Arthur focused on formulating the explanation he would have to give Marshall eventually. For once, his father was not present to give his side of the story, even if his side was often an excuse. Arthur had accepted all his father's excuses, not because he did not know better, but because he hoped one day to make a difference in how the city was managed. He could not do that, if he challenged his father and lost his position as heir.

As they walked through the awakening forest, Arthur could not help realizing there was no excuse he could accept for what his father had done and what his father would try to do to Marshall and possibly Tiana. He was beyond choosing blind obedience, beyond towing his father's line to those who already knew better. He could not see himself returning to the role of dutiful son and ignoring all he had chosen not to see before. Neither did he see himself walking away from the city that had suffered long enough under the rule of mad Hanovers'. He had always intended to become the leader his father was not, to help the city rather than punish it.

Where did that leave him? If he wanted to help the city and repair the damage done by his family, did he not have to return to his father's nest and play the role expected of him?

His eyes went to the back of Marshall's head.

What if returning meant sacrificing his friend and sister?

He could think of only one way to protect them, an option he had not wanted to entertain for weeks.

"Tell me again about this alleged plot to overthrow my father," he spoke quietly.

Marshall glanced over his shoulder at him then back. "Are you addressing me or the wolf?" he snapped through chattering teeth.

Arthur rolled his eyes. "You. I may be willing to talk to your ... friends," he said with effort. "You said there were people who wanted to rid the city of my father."

"You want to betray them to your father."

"No. I want to hear their plan for saving the city from him." Arthur was careful not to advocate for the murder of his father, even though he suspected that was the plan.

Marshall stopped and faced him. "Why?" he asked, gaze sharpening as he studied Arthur. "You have been ignoring me for weeks when I tried to address you on this matter!"

Arthur measured his words before speaking. "I have heard you, even if I did not respond," he said. "Something about our adventure to the forest has changed my perception. I do not disagree with you, Marshall, about the city deserving better than my father."

Marshall's eyebrow lifted. "Suddenly, you do not disagree with me? Does that mean you support what I have said, or are you planning to use this knowledge against me? Or is this a moment of weakness you will regret when we return?"

"Perhaps I have had a vision of what may come to be, if I do not prevent my father from acting as he intends to," Arthur said. "How entrenched is this movement against him? Are you the only one in it?"

"No." Marshall studied him until they both began to

shake harder from the lack of movement. He spun away and began trailing the wolf again.

"Who else is involved?"

Marshall was quiet for a moment.

"I am sorry, Marshall, but I need reassurances this movement has the ability to usurp my father and is not the daydream of the Cruises alone."

"Many powerful men are involved, including my father, and someone close to your father," Marshall replied. His tone had lost its edge. "And … Ingram."

"Gavin Ingram? My father's security advisor?" Arthur had not known if this plan extended beyond the Cruises or not, but the mention of the Ingram patriarch, whose prominent family was the third most influential and wealthiest in the outer city, led him to wonder if it were possible to cultivate Marshall's accomplices as allies. He stood a better chance of outmaneuvering, or outright overthrowing, his father, if so.

Assuming his father did not witness his betrayal in a vision.

"The same," Marshall said.

"Then this plan has deep roots in the elite."

"It does. Very deep. There are more supporters for our plan than your father has supporting him. Four and a half centuries of mad rule is enough," Marshall confirmed slowly. "I am supposed to test you to ensure you were not like your father, then sway you to our side, and if I succeed, introduce you to Ingram and the others upon our return."

"What is your determination? About me?"

"You are arrogant, proud and foolish – but you are not your father."

Arthur did not deny the assessment. In fact, he found it sound, even though it came from a Cruise.

"You are truly interested in usurping your father?" Marshall asked with another uncertain glance towards him.

"I want to protect those I care about and my city," Arthur replied. "If there was a way to do it without challenging my father, I would prefer that."

"And if there is not?"

Arthur hesitated. "I am open to an alternative."

"This is more than I ever thought I would hear you say," Marshall said.

Unable to identify a path where those he cared about lived, and he returned to his duty as the Hanover heir, Arthur lost himself in troubled thought.

They walked until midday. Spring came in full force this day, after the longest winter he could recall. By noon, he was sweating from the heat and sun. Seasonal streams formed as the snow and ice melted, and the forest filled with the movement of animals who no longer feared leaving their burrows. Squirrels leapt from branch to branch above their heads while rabbits rustled in the underbrush.

The she-wolf panted and kept several dozen feet ahead of them, pausing on occasion to ensure they followed. Marshall quietly picked his way through the forest, and Arthur cradled the pups as they walked.

Reaching a stream, they all stopped in silence. Marshall dropped to his knees, cupped his hands and drank from the trickling waters. The she-wolf drank for a moment then approached Arthur. She nudged the pups with her nose. Arthur set them down and unwrapped them while the mother wolf nudged his hands to hasten him. He moved aside for her to inspect the puppies.

"From winter to summer in half a day's time," Marshall complained.

Arthur dunked his head and shivered at the icy water before drinking his fill. "I hope this holds out."

"Me, too."

The she-wolf fed and cleaned her babies. Marshall gathered the tiny wolves and bundled them up again.

Together, the two of them set out once more, following the wolf as she continued north.

Not far past the stream, she stopped abruptly, head elevated.

Arthur and Marshall froze and waited. Her tail stayed down, her ears forward. She did not growl as she had when she saw Ghouls, and she did not appear alarmed.

Shifting their direction, she walked another half a

mile before pausing again at the top of a shallow gully.

Marshall's breath caught, and Arthur hurried to his side.

At the bottom of the gully lay the skinwalker, half man, half beast, unmoving. Two of his limbs were at odd angles. His beast fur was matted with blood and his human skin smeared with it.

The wolf's tail wagged. She trotted down the gully to the still skinwalker and began to lick his bloodied skin.

Marshall cursed.

Arthur was still.

"We should have guessed she would lead us to the beast that's murdered hundreds!" Marshall muttered.

Arthur had a different reaction. "Tiana did that?" he asked, surveying the gashes, crushed body parts, broken limbs and blood of the mangled man.

"Are you not concerned we found the creature that murders entire villages in one breath?" Marshall demanded.

"He can murder no one now," Arthur pointed out.

"Good. I hope he dies here."

"You sound like a Hanover," Arthur said, amused.

Marshall glared at him.

Help him. The she-wolf's whisper was anxious.

Any desire Arthur had to let the skinwalker rot in place was lost when the she-wolf spoke to him. She did not have to ask again, not after saving his life a second time.

"She saved our lives, Marshall, and she brought us here for a reason," Arthur started. "We cannot leave them like this. She is too weak, and he is –"

Before he could finish the sentence, Marshall was striding angrily towards the wolf and skinwalker. "The sooner we are done with this, the sooner we can go home and overthrow your father!" he snapped.

Arthur almost smiled. He asked his magic for help knowing which direction to go in and was pleased with the response. A village belonging to the Newe, their Native allies, was located less than three miles away.

His satisfaction faded when he reached the skinwalker and witnessed his mangled condition firsthand.

The man was alive and blinking, glaring at Arthur and Marshall.

"I ... found ... you again," the Native said in a gravelly voice. His breathing was ragged and irregular, though he displayed no outward sign of pain.

"I believe we found you," Marshall retorted.

Arthur debated how to handle the skinwalker and squatted beside him. "We can help you," he began. "But if we do so, when you are well, you must leave the territory around Lost Vegas for a thousand miles, without causing any further loss of life, and never return. You have hurt too many people."

The skinwalker gave a wheezy laugh.

"You have no room to negotiate right now," Marshall seconded in a hard tone. "I am usually the diplomatic one between the two of us, but for once, I find myself agreeing with a Hanover. Either do as Arthur says, or we leave you here to die."

"I ... agree," wheezed the dangerous Native.

Arthur assessed the beast that was half transformed. "You are a mess," he said. "Can you choose one form? Preferably human, as you will be easier to carry."

The skinwalker closed his eyes.

Arthur waited for a response and then witnessed the beast changing slowly into a naked, fully human form.

"A word," Marshall said to him.

Arthur stood.

Marshall moved a short distance away. "How exactly are we going carry him and the pups? And where are we going to find help? His wounds are beyond our ability to dress without the proper supplies."

"There is a friendly village three miles from here. We can have him there by sunset," Arthur said.

"Sunset? Three miles?"

"We can build a stretcher out of branches."

"And use leaves and fairy magic to bind his wounds?"

Arthur sighed. "Do you have a better idea?"

"I do. One of us goes to the village and asks for help then returns with a healer and enough men to carry him."

"Very well, Cruise. We will adopt your plan," Arthur said, surprised Marshall had an answer that was sound. "Your plan, your choice on who goes to the village."

"I do not want to be left with that thing," Marshall admitted quietly, eyes on the skinwalker. "Agreement or not, I do not trust it. But you have the ability to navigate that I do not."

"Take the she-wolf. She can do what I can."

"Will she leave him and her pups to go with me?"

Arthur approached the wolf, which continued to lick the skinwalker's wounds.

"Would you accompany Marshall to a Native village to fetch help?" Arthur asked the animal, ignoring the native.

The wolf lifted her head.

"You would have to leave your babes and your master. But we need the assistance of the Natives in the village. Marshall can speak to them on your behalf. They are allies of my family," Arthur stated.

The wolf gazed at him for a long moment, not blinking.

"You will be back by the pups' suppertime," Marshall added. "I cannot navigate the forest alone, and we cannot leave your pups and master exposed. One of us must stay. Arthur is more adept than I at treating the wounded. He is a Hanover. He does not mind blood on his hands."

Arthur rolled his eyes.

The she-wolf looked between them then at the

skinwalker.

Yes, she answered.

Arthur nodded to Marshall.

"Do you know the place you seek?" Arthur asked the animal. He formed a vision of the path and the destination.

Without answering him, the wolf spun and loped in the direction of the village.

Marshall hurried after her.

Arthur watched them go and then moved closer to the skinwalker. He sat down on a log and placed the bundle on the ground between them.

"How are they?" the skinwalker wheezed.

"Healthy from what I know," Arthur replied. He peeled off his shirt and began tearing it into strips. "How is it our paths continue to cross?"

"You ... hunted me," the skinwalker responded. "I hunted you."

"You hunted me?" Arthur asked. "You did not seem interested in me when I was stalking you all those days."

"Did not know ... your name."

"Ah. You did not think my father would allow his heir to wander the forest like a lost dog. The secret is, he did not know." After a quick assessment, Arthur shifted forward to bind the worst of the wounds. He started with the Native's right leg and then paused. "Have you always been missing your left leg?"

"It will return."

Arthur studied the skinwalker's features. They were tight, and an unhealthy gray shaded half his face. "Because it is magic," he said. The skinwalker was the man in the world he least wanted as a companion, but as long as the creature continued talking, he would not fall asleep and die from his substantial head wounds. "The legend I heard claims your magic lives in your leg." Arthur shifted forward to look at the stump. "This was not a wound. You were born deformed?"

The skinwalker did not answer.

Arthur moved on to the other wounds. When he ran out of shirt, he removed the pups from their cloak and tore it in half. He left half for the pups and ripped the rest into strips.

"Who did this to you?" he asked, wanting to hear someone other than Tiana had.

"A little girl with Ghoul eyes."

Arthur was quiet for a moment. "I did not know she was capable of this."

"You know her?"

"My sister. The one you swore not to harm."

The Native gave another rattling, shaky laugh. "I have been lying here … planning her death. Nothing has given me … this much pleasure in years."

"Unfortunately for you, you already agreed to spare her," Arthur reminded him. His thoughts went briefly to the changed vision.

The Native grimaced as Arthur cinched tight one of his wounds.

"I do not know how she could do this to any living creature or how you are alive at all."

"She did not want me dead ... or ... I'd be dead," the skinwalker said.

"There is that." Arthur's hands paused, and he recalled what Tiana had told him about murdering Marshall's sister, who had been Tiana's stepmother. Had her first experience wielding her power scared her out of murdering anyone else? "I hunted you, because I had visions of you killing her. How is that possible when she can do something like this?" The question was more for him than the skinwalker.

To his surprise, the skinwalker answered. "What did you see? Exactly? Tell me again."

Arthur's hands paused. He remembered how interested the skinwalker had seemed when he mentioned the vision before, at the frozen river. He began to wipe and bind the wounds again.

"You were chasing her across the grasslands ..." Arthur murmured and told him the scene he had witnessed nightly for months. When he finished, the skinwalker was silent.

Arthur shifted forward to ensure the man still lived.

"Then you did not see me kill her," the skinwalker

said.

"No, but why else would you be pursuing her?" And why was their father now in the vision?

"I do not know," the skinwalker admitted. "But what you saw was … what you saw. It was not more or less than this."

"You think I should not assume you were trying to hurt her?"

"What you saw was what you saw."

The skinwalker had a point, and Arthur was not certain he liked taking advice from a beast that had slaughtered every living being in three villages.

"You said you were hunting me?" he asked. "Why?"

"Paid to hunt people."

"Who paid you?"

The skinwalker smiled.

Arthur's family had never been beloved. His father uncovered at least one plot a year to assassinate him and another to assassinate his heir. "For once, I do not blame someone for wanting my family dead," he said, thoughts on Marshall.

"He wanted you … alive."

"Ransom is a good motivation as well. My family is wealthy, and my father powerful," he said. "Who is this man? How did he come to have enough money to tempt anyone to kidnap a Hanover?"

"My price is never money," the skinwalker reminded

him.

"He must have had something of value."

"Every man has something of value."

Arthur waited, dissatisfied with the response. When the skinwalker did not elaborate, he pressed for an answer. "Where were you supposed to take me, assuming you succeeded?"

"Not far from here."

"So he is local."

The skinwalker was quiet.

"Does it matter now who it is?" Arthur prodded. "You have failed. Why not tell me?"

"It is not a matter of failure that keeps me quiet," snapped the skinwalker moodily. "You will not believe me if I reveal who he is."

Arthur leaned forward in interest. "Who is it?"

"A man with a mark like the one you bear."

Arthur touched his shoulder, where the tattoo of an eagle was located. The sacred mark was born only by Hanover's. "My father?" he asked, surprised.

"No."

"No one else bears this mark, except for my sister."

"I told you. You would not believe me."

It was hard to think when his mind was fatigued and his body starving, but Arthur could only draw one conclusion. "Another Hanover? One outside the city?"

"He tracked me down when I was two thousand miles

away," the skinwalker explained. "Hired me without asking my price."

"Interesting tale, but to my knowledge, no other Hanover is alive at the moment. Who was it really?"

The skinwalker muttered something under his breath and dropped his head back, falling silent.

Sensing he was done speaking on the topic, Arthur tried another topic to encourage him to stay awake. "Your wolf. How did you come by her?"

"Not wolf. Guide."

"Guide? She leads you places and you murder everyone in them?" Arthur asked, confused.

The skinwalker laughed hoarsely. "No. She is my spirit guide."

"From the spirit world."

"Yes."

"Hmm. A spirit wolf. Well, I cannot deny she is no normal animal."

"She has been too weak to heal or travel far," the skinwalker said.

"Her pups are spirit babies?"

"One may be. It is rare for more than … one to possesses the gift she does."

Arthur looked at the pile of warm, fuzzy puppies. "Is their father a wolf or spirit or … you?" he asked.

"No father."

"Interesting." Arthur finished binding the last of the

major wounds and sat back. "Knowing what you do now of my sister, why do you think you were in my vision?"

"You said I was in this form for most of the visions."

"That is correct."

The skinwalker gazed at the blue sky visible through the pine needle canopy above. "I rarely kill in this form," he said at last.

"You do not believe you were pursuing her to kill her."

"No."

"Why else would you be pursuing her?"

"It was your ... vision. Not mine."

Arthur dwelled on this tidbit of information. The discussion changed his initial interpretation of visions he had of the skinwalker chasing Tiana. He was less clear as to why his father would be in a field outside the city, since no Hanover leader ever left the city after ascending to his place in charge, but his father's fury was unmistakable.

"After you promised not to hurt her, when we were at the river, the visions ceased," Arthur said. "I cannot imagine you were not chasing her for good reasons. Thus your promise must have stopped that version of her future. I did nothing else in the span of that day to affect it."

"Maybe she did."

"For a murderous beast, you are rather wise," Arthur stated reluctantly.

"I have lived … two, maybe three lifetimes. You owe me for granting this promise," the skinwalker reminded me. "More so after your sister tried to tear me apart."

"I will uphold my side of the deal," Arthur said. "What is it you want?"

"I will tell you when the time is right."

Uneasiness twisted Arthur's empty stomach. The skinwalker had not said he would reveal the price when he decided what it was. Which meant, he already knew. What was he waiting for? Did he have visions as well?

What could a man evil enough to slaughter babes in their mothers' arms possibly want from Arthur?

Who is worse – this man or my father? Arthur contemplated with no small amount of surprise his father had competition.

The skinwalker's eyes closed.

"You must stay awake. I do not care if you die, but our common friend does. She has been too good to me for me not to act in her favor." Arthur gathered up the pups and shifted back to the log. "What is your given name? I have heard several variations."

"The man who bore … my given name is dead. I call myself Black Wolf, in honor of my guide."

"You murdered my friends, Black Wolf," Arthur said. "Good men. Men I have known my entire life."

"They are here with me."

"What?"

35

Black Wolf smiled coldly. "All the spirits ... all *my* spirits ... they stay with me forever. Say farewell, if you wish. Your friends are standing behind you."

Arthur whipped around without seeing anyone. He relaxed. "You are hallucinating."

"You believe in your magic but not mine," the skinwalker observed.

"Your magic is terrifying. Nonetheless, you have lost too much blood not to be delirious." With no food for two days, Arthur was growing too uncomfortable to continue the discussion. He huddled with the pups on the log, feeling ill himself.

The skinwalker's eyes closed once more, and his breathing became deeper.

"Awake." Arthur nudged him with his foot.

Black Wolf's eyes opened again.

"My ... friend," Arthur started. "One of those you attacked. He did not die, but from my understanding, he is badly wounded. My sister claims you inflicted him with a wound that will not heal."

"Maybe."

"It is not outside the possible?"

"If I hurt him in this form, the wound is like any other," the skinwalker explained. "If I was in my other forms, then the wound was made with magic."

"How is a magical wound healed?"

"Only I can heal it."

"And in return, you would want something from me," Arthur said. "If I promise to pay it, will you heal it?"

The skinwalker peered at him closely for a moment then relaxed his head to the ground once more. "No."

"No? Why not?" Arthur prodded, mind on Warner and what Tiana had revealed about his lover's condition.

"When I reveal the price for not killing your sister, you will understand. It's rare when anyone can afford my services twice."

A chill ran through Arthur. "I would do anything for him."

"You may have the opportunity to prove this."

What could Black Wolf ask of him that would make him unwilling to pay a second time?

It seemed too simple for the price to be his life. Why would the skinwalker hide it if so?

Arthur surveyed the skinwalker's body, not at all convinced the creature would survive until sundown. With his attention split between Black Wolf and his own misery, he shifted to sit on the ground with his back to the log and rested his head back. The pups stilled soon after he did. He began to doze fitfully and soon forgot his efforts to keep the creature awake.

No visions formed, and the hunger in his belly turned to pain.

No more than three hours later, however, he felt the warm lick of a rough tongue against his cheek and opened his eyes. Too distracted by his own misery, he had not heard the wolf's approach.

"Hi there," he said and shifted to sit up straight. As if sensing their mother, the pups began to squirm. She nudged the bundle. Arthur set it down and then glanced around. "I hope you brought help."

Slow. She replied and then settled onto the ground beside him to feed her babies. Her fur was marbled black and white.

Arthur rose and went still, overcome by dizziness. When the spell passed, he returned to the skinwalker's side. "Are you dead?" he asked.

"Not … yet." Black Wolf's eyes cracked open.

"I would recommend you not reveal your identity as a skinwalker," Arthur advised with some amusement. "You decimated one of the Newe villages."

Black Wolf grunted in response.

"Arthur!" Marshall's call came from several hundred feet away. "I lost the damn wolf!"

"Here, Marshall," Arthur croaked loudly.

Minutes later, the Cruise heir appeared, trailed by four Natives. Marshall had been provided a change of clothes and carried a satchel across his chest. He reached Arthur and pulled the satchel off to hand to him.

"I brought their healer and people to carry him," Marshall reported.

Arthur reached into the satchel and felt a canteen and

something wrapped in canvas. He pulled it out, smelling the food before he opened it and unwrapped it to reveal a thick venison sandwich on flatbread.

He ate it as fast as he could, oblivious to the movement and discussion going on around him. When he was done, he drank all the water in the canteen and lowered it then threw his head back with a satisfied sigh.

"I could eat a herd of buffalo," he said.

Marshall moved closer to him. "They were reluctant to help. I promised them our fathers would compensate them well."

Arthur nodded. "I can imagine our allies are uncomfortable, given the recent events. Skinwalkers, Hanover's …" He shook his head.

"The Natives believe your father means to burn the forest down to find his heirs," Marshall said. "Even our Newe allies are preparing for possible war."

Arthur watched the healer strip off the skinwalker's bandages, clean the wounds, and re-bandage them. Two of the Natives stood waiting with a stretcher.

"I know you wish to find your sister, but we need to return before your father does something rash," Marshall urged him. "The Natives claim the smoke from the city is so thick, it hides the city at dawn and dusk, and he is calling in favors from every ally he has to amass weapons and food."

Arthur listened, his stomach sinking. Even he did not

know what his unpredictable father would do in this circumstance. The Hanover hold on the city would be threatened by the loss of both his children, and the political challenges were likely to mount. Tiana was safe outside the city, as safe as she could be. Arthur could return safely, but Marshall could not, and he would not allow the fiery fate to befall his friend. Not yet, until Arthur had bargained for Marshall's life or found support among his father's detractors.

Arthur glanced down at the pups, which were being cleaned by their mother, then at the men loading the skinwalker onto the stretcher. "We both need rest and food. We can discuss our plans to leave in the morning," he said, aware Marshall was waiting for his decision.

"Your sister will be safe. She can take care of herself," Marshall said, sensing his hesitation.

Arthur nodded. He did not believe for one second he should abandon Tiana, no matter how many people claimed she had great powers. But neither did he want Marshall's compassion directed at *him*. The guilt sliding through him was enough without his friend's understanding look.

He moved away from Marshall to gather the pups. The wolf stood and then carefully watched over the men carefully moving her master. Arthur cradled the pups and fell into step behind Marshall, ahead of the stretcher, and behind the Native leading them back towards the village.

His stomach growled again, but he did not hear it, not when his mind was raging between telling Marshall the truth and leaving before the Cruise heir could stop him. He could not save his friend and sister unless he reached his father before either of them.

CHAPTER THREE

AVELINE AWOKE RAVENOUS AND FEVERED. Sweat rolled down the sides of her face, and she pushed off the blankets trapping her to the narrow bed. One of her arms was heavy, clumsy, probably wounded, though she experienced no pain anywhere.

"Finally," Tiana's soft exclamation was followed by the touch of her cool palms against Aveline's cheeks.

It was not the warmth of her surroundings alone that caused Aveline's discomfort, but the eerie charge radiating off Tiana, usually present when she used magic or was agitated. Her head throbbed, and her thoughts were laced with the heaviness indicative of some medicines.

"Air," Aveline croaked. She opened her eyes – and saw only darkness.

The charge lessened, and she heard Tiana shift and move around her. Seconds later, a cool breeze touched the exposed skin of her legs and feet.

"Am I blind?" Aveline asked.

Tiana laughed. She lifted a cloth off Aveline's face.

Aveline blinked rapidly. She didn't feel hurt or tired – but something was off about her body. Tiana's smile distracted her. The Hanover girl sported a yellow bruise around one eye and along one cheek and wore the traditional dress of the Native enemies of the city: fleece, fur and leather.

A Native peered down at Aveline with a sharp, assessing gaze, leaving her with no doubt this was a healer.

"Can you sit?" the middle-aged woman asked.

Aveline did so, frowning when she caught herself careening to the side of her heavy arm. She steadied herself and looked around. She was inside a small, round tent that smelled of herbs. The tent flap was pinned open, and she glimpsed the cloudy sky and trees outside.

She shook off the blanket covering her arm.

"Wait!" Tiana stretched across her to stop her from flinging off the blanket completely.

Aveline stilled, but Tiana did not let her go.

"What do you remember last?" Tiana asked her, black gaze studying her closely.

Aveline thought back. "Jose, Rocky and I arrived here

and … there was a commotion." Most of her memories were a blur after arriving to the encampment. "I remember feeling hot and sick during our travels and more so when we arrived. Am I diseased? What happened?"

"You are suffering from a deformity," the healer said.

"You transformed into a skinwalker," Tiana said simultaneously.

Aveline looked between the two of them. "What?"

"Half skinwalker," Tiana corrected herself. "Leaving the city may have caused you to try to transform. But because you are only half skinwalker, you could not transform fully. Your body tried and it almost killed you."

Aveline started to laugh. "Have you been reading your fairy tales again?" she asked.

"No, Aveline. I am very serious," Tiana said. "But you know what this means? We are both very special. I always knew you were and now I know why." She appeared pleased.

"I'm not deformed. I'm not magical. I'm not …" Aveline lifted her heavy arm as she spoke and reached up to scratch her head.

From the elbow down, her arm resembled that of a bear, down to the massive paw and four inch talons.

She stared.

"You have to stay calm!" Tiana said. She hurried around the bed and draped the blanket over her arm again. "You cannot change on your own, but your body tries when you are distressed."

Aveline stared at the blanket, unable to believe what she had seen. She began to tense, and panic fluttered through her. As if in response, thick fur crept up her expanding bicep.

"Calm," Tiana said again.

Aveline met her gaze.

The Hanover girl was not at all alarmed by the sight of her deformed arm.

"Tiana, what's wrong with me?" Aveline managed.

"Nothing," Tiana said firmly. "We are both special. Did your father or mother not murder a thousand people in three days?"

Aveline nodded and swallowed hard.

"This is how. As a skinwalker. You are only half, so you are not transforming fully. When you had nightmares, half of you turned into a bear and the other half either remained human or turned into a great cat," Tiana explained. "It was quite confusing for us."

Aveline shook off the blanket again and lifted her bear claw. She flexed her hand and then released, dismayed when the bear paw responded to her commands as if it were really her hand. She squeezed it closed.

"It will make you an even better assassin," Tiana added. "You can cleave a person in two with one hand."

Aveline was silent. Deep down inside, next to the

panic subdued by pain medication, was the acknowledgement of what she had always known: she was different. She had spent her life aware of her devil's blood and the curse she inherited, without ever expecting it to manifest into her physical body.

"Do you not agree?" Tiana asked. "Your claws are larger than my fingers." She took the paw in both hand and tugged Aveline's fist open to display the talons. Aveline felt her cool palms again, this time through the fur and skin of her bear claw.

It really was *her*.

"I guess it will make me more effective," Aveline allowed. "But how do I live a normal life with this?" She waved the bear paw. "I'm deformed!"

Tiana's smile was warm, understanding. Peering into the Hanover girl's Ghoulish eyes, Aveline realized what she had said.

"I didn't mean … Tiana, you've always wanted to leave the city anyway, to go somewhere where you would fit in. I just want to stay in Lost Vegas and be like my father," Aveline said weakly. "I cannot exactly blend into a crowd with a hand like this. I am sorry if I hurt your feelings, Tiana, but I don't want to be deformed."

"You did not," Tiana assured her. "You are appalled to be different, but I am happy not to be alone anymore. I am happy my closest friend is like me. I am the selfish one. I should apologize to you."

Tiana Hanover did not have a selfish bone in her body, and Aveline knew it.

"You can wear a glove," Tiana suggested.

This time, Aveline reviewed what she wanted to say before speaking. There was no hiding a deformity this size and no glove that would accommodate four-inch claws. The transformation turned her lower arm from its normal size to the thickness of her thigh. "Maybe," she said for Tiana's sake.

"We are like sisters now," Tiana said and smiled again.

Aveline had a hard time finding any good in her circumstances. It would take a lot of work to hide her deformity in the city, where she was likely to be burnt at the stakes by Tiana's father, if discovered. With another look at Tiana's smile, Aveline kept her concerns quiet and studied her massive paw.

Tiana was right about being able to slash a person into pieces, she admitted. It would help her coerce people into doing or saying what she wanted. People like the man who betrayed her.

Aware of Tiana's hopeful gaze, Aveline released the breath she held and nodded. The fur crept down her arm, and her bicep returned to its normal size. "This can be useful," she said. "Once I'm used to it."

She did not need to look at Tiana to feel the Hanover girl's excitement.

"Where are my clothes?" she asked and glanced down. She was naked beneath the blankets.

"You have been sleeping for two days. Every time you transformed, you tore apart the clothing you wore," Tiana explained and twisted to see the healer. "Will you examine her again?"

Aveline gritted her teeth in irritation. She was headachy and groggy from the medication the healer had given her. The skin of her bicep started to stretch again in response to her emotion. Forcing herself to relax, she sat with tried patience as the healer examined her quickly.

With a brisk nod, the Native moved away from her.

Tiana stood waiting, Native clothing in her arms. She appeared comfortable, if not outright cheerful, dressed like one of the Diné who had declared war on her family and Lost Vegas.

"My clothing is shredded?" Aveline asked.

"It is," Tiana said and rested the Native clothing on the bed. "But you are one of them. You will fit right in."

Aveline eyed the garb without moving.

"Was your mother not a Native?" Tiana prodded.

Aware both of them were watching her, Aveline nodded. "She died at my birth," she said. *Allegedly.*

Leaving the city had been worse than she ever expected it to be. She had begun to doubt the foundation of her life and now, she was deformed. She had always known the devil's blood ran through her veins. Was this what her father had tried to tell her? Why he taught her to control her anger never to lash out at anyone? Was skinwalking the devil's curse? If so, why had he not told her directly what would happen, if she did not control her emotions?

Why had he never transformed into a beast form in front of her to show her what form her fate would take?

Rocky's insistence that Aveline's mother did not die at birth returned, along with the claim her mother – not her father, as she had been told – had been the one possessed by devil's blood who massacred a thousand people in three days.

She did not want to believe her father would lie to her.

"The skinwalker tribe is said to come from the far north," the Native was saying. "Your mother was far from her people."

Why would her father keep this truth from her, too?

Aveline flung off her blankets. "Yeah, well, maybe she realized skinwalkers are terrible people," she said. She dressed quickly. "Where are Jose and Rocky?"

"They are safe," Tiana said. "Everyone is in this village, except for Arthur and Marshall Cruise."

"Is your brother well?" Aveline asked.

"I believe so," she replied. "I had a vision of him last night. He is alive."

"And *you*?"

"Their chief has been very kind to me," Tiana replied. "They hate my father, too."

Aveline snorted. "But are you free to leave? A prisoner?"

"They are being unnecessarily kind, considering whose daughter I am," Tiana said.

Aveline's instincts, honed by learning to survive the streets, were nowhere near as assured or calm as Tiana's. Even if the Hanover patriarch did not want his deformed daughter back, he would use her to get what he wanted, and so would his mortal enemies. Tiana was at ease and smiling, as if she were a guest, but Aveline guessed that was far from the case, especially since Arthur was no longer in this tribe's possession.

"You even have a feather," Aveline murmured, uncertain why she was disturbed to see Tiana in the clothing of her enemies. The feather was pinned in Tiana's hair, a streak of black against the blond.

"I earned it," Tiana said quietly, solemnly.

Aveline's eyebrows quirked in amusement. "What you have done?"

"I took a life."

Aveline knew nothing of the Natives' traditions and wondered why Tiana had revealed killing Matilda to anyone. Her head ached too much for her to think clearly about everything. "If you want to wear it, then do it," she said. "If they are forcing you to, then don't."

"They have not forced me to do anything."

"I find it hard to believe you are being treated well by your father's enemies."

"You will see. Their chief is very kind," Tiana added. "He requested to speak to you when you were awake, if you feel well enough?"

"Definitely," Aveline said, suspecting she was going to have to help Tiana navigate the politics of this place.

"Thank you," Tiana said to the healer.

Aveline followed her out of the tent into the village. Tiana had no chains, no one watching her at all that Aveline could find. The Hanover girl moved through the village unchallenged and paused outside the largest of the temporary tents located towards the center of the village.

"Sir?" she called. "Aveline is awake."

After a pause, the entrance was flung open by a Native not much older than Rocky.

For the first time, Aveline saw Tiana wilt, as she often had in the city. Her eyes dropped, shoulders hunched, and she stepped aside.

I hate that, Aveline thought. The fur on her bear arm expanded, and she forced herself to breathe deeply.

"Come," the Native said curtly to Aveline.

Already disliking him, Aveline nonetheless obeyed and entered the warm tent. Tiana remained outside, and the flap closed behind her. A fire and a single bulb lit the interior enough for Aveline to see the form of an elderly man seated near the fire. He was bundled in blankets despite the overly warm tent.

"It pleases me to see you well," the older man said and peered up at her.

Aveline started to cross her arms and then stopped when her bear claw interfered. "Am I a prisoner?" she asked.

"You are a guest, until my father decides otherwise," the younger man said in a hard tone. "He wishes to speak to you about the Hanover girl."

Here comes the bad news, Aveline thought and braced herself to learn that Tiana had been lied to.

"Please, sit in comfort," the older man seconded and motioned to a spot near him. "I am Elk Hunter. This is my son, Diving Eagle. We have much to discuss." He paused and coughed hard enough for his face to turn bright red.

Diving Eagle handed him a wooden goblet of water.

"You are her guardian, are you not?" the elderly man asked when he had recovered.

"I am," Aveline replied. "Appointed by her brother and father."

"You entered my village subversively."

She said nothing.

"I wish to speak to you openly about the circumstances you both find yourselves in. I value your honesty."

Aveline hesitated then sat opposite him. "My friends?

Jose and Rocky? Are they in these same circumstances?" she asked.

"Jose is an ally, and claims Rocky is his protector," the chief said. "How true this is does not concern me. What concerns me most is the Hanover in our midst. Your friends will remain here, pending your agreement to our terms, and the Hanover carrying out what she has agreed to already."

"They're hostages."

"Yes."

Aveline swallowed hard. "She is nothing like her father or her brother," Aveline said. "She will keep whatever promise you forced her into making. Your grievances could not be directed toward a more innocent person."

"I am aware she is different," Elk Hunter acknowledged. "And we all saw what she did to the skinwalker."

Aveline's brow quirked. In the far reaches of her mind, she saw an image of a Native man and a wolf, a flurry of movement, someone shouting … but none of the pictures formed completely. "I can't remember anything," she said.

Elk Hunter glanced at his son, who began to speak.

Aveline listened to his version of events, of Tiana using magic to subdue and then throw the skinwalker into the sky, in quiet. She recalled Matilda's death at Tiana's hands, and the magical events Tiana could not control, the telekinesis and mind reading.

"You are not surprised," Elk Hunter observed, sharp eyes on her.

"No," Aveline replied.

"Would it surprise you to know only one Hanover heir every generation is born with this power, which allows him to rule and protect his city?"

Aveline frowned. "But Arthur is the Hanover heir, not Tiana."

"This is clearly what their father used to believe as well," Elk Hunter said. "Though he must have suspected otherwise to assign you as her guardian and to send the messages I have been receiving lately."

"Perhaps he *hopes* otherwise," Diving Eagle said.

Aveline tensed. "Why would you say that?" she snapped.

"Because her mind is not fit to lead," he replied.

She rose. Anger flared within her, warming her body from the inside out. Her shirtsleeve ripped as her entire arm transformed into that of a bear. "There is *nothing* wrong with Tiana!" she growled.

The warrior shifted closer, eyes flashing with challenge.

"My son means no disrespect," Elk Hunter said with a glance at his edgy Native son. "His anger is derived from a different source."

The warrior looked at his father and then dipped his head. "My apologies, Father," he said through gritted teeth. "I did not mean it as an insult. The Hanover views the world through her heart."

"That's a good thing!" Aveline retorted.

"I would agree," Elk Finder said. "It's a gift to view the world as beautiful when most of us see its faults instead."

"But you must admit she cannot do so, if she is to lead," his son said reasserted more quietly.

"Soon, you will see things as I do," his father replied with a warm smile.

"No, Father. You will live many years yet and lead us through what the Hanover's bring upon us."

Aveline half-listened, assessing the elderly chief was too frail to survive the year. Deep inside, she understood Tiana's chances of survival on her own were not good. The Hanover girl was too gentle to use her power to hurt others, which left Aveline puzzled about Tiana's motivation for trying to murder a skinwalker.

Aveline scratched her neck with her normal hand and felt the fur that had spread across her shoulder and up her neck. She grimaced. Holding her temper had always been a challenge. She now had an additional reason to work harder at it.

"Please, sit. We are here to discuss her fate, and yours," the chief said.

The words settled some of Aveline's fury, as she

realized the importance of this casual meeting. If she reacted poorly, she likely condemned them all. Rolling her shoulders back, she sat back down.

"You are aware of the nature of the relationship between my people and the Hanover's?" Elk Hunter asked her.

Aveline nodded.

"You understand, then, that I cannot release her." He glanced at his son again. "My behavior towards the daughter of the enemy of my people has been lenient enough for my own people to doubt me. She is being treated as an honored guest and has her freedom, as long as she remains within the village. After witnessing what the skinwalker did to another of our villages, this one filled with families and children, I did not believe it right to confine her after she prevented the skinwalker from doing the same to this village." He shifted and sipped water before continuing. "Those outside the village, who did not witness her actions, do not understand how I could grant our enemy life, let alone regard her as a guest. The tribal council arrives today to review my decisions, and I have entrusted them with a recommendation, and ultimate decision, of how to handle both of you."

Aveline listened, startled by his candidness. Her arm returned to normal, until her bear claw was all that remained of her deformity. "Why are you telling me this?" she asked warily.

"I am recommending Tiana's life be spared, under three conditions."

Aveline braced herself for the bad news. "What are they?"

"The first, that she helps us trap the skinwalker."

"I thought you said it was thrown into the sky," she said.

"It landed five miles away – alive. Barely, if the amount of blood found around its landing place is any indication," Elk Hunter replied. "However, his body was not there. As long as the creature is loose in our lands, and we hunt it, our focus is elsewhere than on our traditional enemy, who becomes a larger threat each day."

"You want her to capture it?" Aveline asked.

"We will track it, but only she can contain it," Diving Eagle said.

"Why not kill it?"

"We intend to use it against our enemy."

Aveline was not at all opposed to witnessing a skinwalker kill – or try to – the Hanover leader. "That man will not die easily," she said. "I don't think even a skinwalker can stop his madness. But I will not stop you from trying. After all he has done to the city and to his own daughter ..." She shook her head.

"You will have the ability to speak to it as well," Diving Eagle said.

"I don't care to."

"Don't you wish to understand more of what you are as well? It can teach you about your mother's people and your heritage," he pointed out.

"I don't want to know more," Aveline snapped. "I am content knowing what I do and carrying on my father's legacy. Now, what's the second condition?"

"That she and her successors will never harm a member of our people."

"Basically, peace with a Hanover," Aveline said. "What of her brother?"

"We did not have a chance to discuss this with him before he vanished. But when we have him again, he will agree to similar terms, or they both die," replied the warrior firmly.

It was not hard for Aveline to believe the siblings would have no problem agreeing to peace, unlike their mad father.

She heard the soft patter of rain begin to fall against the tent and looked upward.

Had Tiana ever been out in the rain? The errant thought distracted her, made the silence stretch uncomfortably. "What's the third condition?" she asked and refocused.

"She can never return to the city," Elk Hunter replied.

"I'm sure she didn't argue with you there, either. She's always wanted to ..." Aveline stopped suddenly, registering the condition. As Tiana's guardian, if the

Hanover girl did not return, neither could she.

"You anticipate a problem?"

"Not with her," she answered. "Do these conditions apply to me as well?"

"They do," Elk Hunter confirmed. "You are part skinwalker, a danger as great as either Hanover."

"You want to banish us."

"That is the goal," Diving Eagle said. "In exchange, you and the Hanover live."

"It is more than I ever thought I would offer a Hanover," his father said.

"I am not a Hanover," Aveline retorted. "Tiana does not belong anywhere her father can reach her, but I belong in that city. It's my home."

The two were silent.

"You of all people understand what it means to want vengeance," she continued. "You have not walked away from a war spanning centuries! The man who betrayed my father and me remains in Lost Vegas, and I *will* find him!"

The warrior shifted at last and approached his father. He bent and whispered quietly before straightening once more. Elk Hunter appeared to think on the request before he nodded.

Diving Eagle looked at her hard. "She can never return. You may, if you agree to carry out our business inside the city," he said.

"Business?" she repeated.

"You are an assassin?"

In training. Though no one seemed to care she was not an official member of the Guild.

Aveline nodded.

"And a skinwalker. You would stand a better chance of surviving an assassination on the Hanover chief than any others we have sent to subvert him."

Aveline had never heard of any Native challenging Tiana's father but doubted said Native would have gotten far before he ran into someone who decided to burn him at the stake. Surviving Lost Vegas was an art in and of itself. A stranger to the city would not know that.

"You will be given ten days," Elk Hunter said solemnly.

"Ten days?" Aveline echoed. "Most assassinations take months to plan!"

"If you fail, Tiana's life is forfeit," Diving Eagle said. "As are yours and those of your friends."

It was a compromise of sorts, one that would allow her to enter the city again, even if she carried the burden of executing vengeance on behalf of complete strangers. Then again, was that not what she had always wanted to do? Become a professional assassin? Why did this feel like more strings were attached than would be in a paid job?

Her life, Rocky's, Jose's and Tiana's were in the hands of the men awaiting her answer, people who, for reasons she did not fully understand, seemed to genuinely wish to spare them. What made the mortal enemies – who were involved in a centuries' old blood feud with Tiana's family – risk angering their own people to protect the Hanover girl?

Because she's special. Aveline had always understood this, but something other than her heavy bear claw felt off about this situation.

"I have no real choice here," Aveline said. "I'll do what you ask."

"You are wise for someone so young." Elk Hunter smiled. "We cannot take the city while he is in charge." He exchanged a look with his son. "The Hanover agreed already to the three conditions. Before you leave for the city, you will both have to testify before the council this evening."

"We have to see the council?"

"They will be interviewing everyone in the village, including you."

"Are you certain you should send her?" Aveline asked. "Tiana will only tell the truth, and if your people are angry with you for treating her well, they might be even angrier when they see the extent of it."

"The truth is expected," the chief said.

The rain fell harder against the leather ceiling of the tent.

Elk Hunter began to cough again and was soon

doubled over.

"You're dismissed," Diving Eagle snapped at her and dropped to his father's side.

Aveline glared at him again before whirling and striding out. She clenched her bear paw and shifted her weight. Her unnatural hand was heavy enough she had to constantly correct her posture to keep from overcompensating and leaning.

The rain was cold and dashed what warmth the early spring day had held. Aveline shivered. As she mentally reviewed the discussion with the chief and his son, dread slid through her.

Had they manipulated her into a suicide mission? Had she let her emotion cloud her judgment?

Did it matter? Not only did she have no choice, but Aveline always intended to return to the city.

Aveline had promised to help Tiana, and breaking this promise would dishonor her father and everything he stood for.

But … Aveline had always suspected the biggest threat to Tiana was her father. Someone wealthy enough to pay off Karl had tried to hire her to murder Tiana anyway. Who was in a better position than Tiana's father?

Unable to make sense of her situation through her headache, Aveline sighed.

Tiana had not gone far from the tent. She stood near the bonfires located at the center of the village with a scrawny Native boy whose head reached her shoulder. They were hand-in-hand, their faces tilted upwards towards the sky, as if they both enjoyed the rain Tiana had never felt against her skin.

"Views the world through her heart."

Aveline had not heard the chief's son follow her but turned when he spoke. "That will never be a bad thing," she told him.

"Not for her. Perhaps for those around her," Diving Eagle retorted. "If she loses her faith in the world, she will destroy everything she touches."

His words left Aveline colder than the rain. She could think of no comeback and watched him stalk away. The Native's glance lingered on the two figures enjoying the rain before he barked an order. The boy with Tiana dashed to him in response, and the two left Aveline's line of sight.

The longer she stood in thought, the more she understood his words. He saw the threat Tiana could become, if she ever saw the darker side of life. Tiana could become something worse than her father.

Except Aveline knew what Diving Eagle did not: Tiana had lived in the shadows her entire life and still glowed with light, hope and optimism. The shadows had not tamed and twisted her spirit. The darker the experiences, the brighter Tiana would glow, the way the moon overpowered the light of stars, no matter how dark the night.

The only danger to Tiana, if her abilities were as powerful as the chief claimed, was the fear of men who misunderstood her – and her father.

Aveline approached Tiana, concerned and overwhelmed by the complexity of their situation.

"I have never felt rain on my face before," Tiana said. "Is it not wonderful?"

"It's cold," Aveline said grumpily. Her irritation could not dampen Tiana's excitement at her world, and the Hanover girl stretched out her arms, as if trying to drench herself in water. "We need to talk about something. Where is Rocky?"

"This way!" Tiana whirled and began walking back towards the direction they had come.

Aveline trailed. She found herself more troubled about what was to come than how she could ever pass as normal sporting a bear claw.

Tiana waited for her at the front of a tent. Rocky emerged and caught Aveline's gaze. He inclined his head to the side.

"I need to talk to Rocky," Aveline said to Tiana. "Stay right here. I'll be right back."

Joining Rocky, the two of them walked a short distance away.

"How are you?" Rocky asked, searching her features.

"I feel like I fell out of a tree." Aveline touched her

pounding head. "Is it true what I've been told? Tiana tried to murder someone?"

"It was pretty impressive," Rocky said with a smile. His eyes went from her to a passing Native. "I have the feeling we're in trouble here."

"We are. Lots of it," she agreed. "They want me to kill someone in the city. In exchange, they won't hurt any of you."

"Sounds suspicious to me."

She nodded, eyes on the forest. "None of this feels right." She lifted her bear claw. "I want to find Karl but not like this."

"Go," Rocky said easily. "I can take care of your friend."

"I made her a promise. My father would not approve of me leaving her."

"Then come back," Rocky said. "Nothing will happen to her while I'm here. You deserve closure, Avi."

She had not expected him to agree with her. "You haven't heard who they want me to kill yet," she said ruefully.

Rocky waited.

The second she said his name, his expression changed from open to shuttered.

Rocky listened, concern on his face, as she filled him in on the conversation that had transpired with the chief and his son.

When she was done, Rocky rocked back onto his heels and gazed towards the clouds.

"What would you do?" Aveline asked. Never had she had to ask this question of anyone.

"You have ten days?"

She nodded.

"Don't worry about anything out here," Rocky said. "Find Karl. His brother Wilhelm lives in the old place where Karl used to live. You remember visiting him there when we were little?"

"Yes."

"Get what you need from Wilhelm and Karl, and you meet me in nine days. I'll bring Tiana and Jose, and we'll all go somewhere."

"You don't think I should try to kill the Hanover leader at all?" Aveline asked.

"I think every assassin who has tried to kill a siting Hanover leader for four centuries has failed for a reason," Rocky replied.

"Would you try?"

"No."

Surprised by his quick, honest response, Aveline considered her position on the matter. All she had ever wanted was to follow in her father's footsteps. What better way than by murdering the Hanover leader?

"What if ..." She looked at her bear claw. "What if I'm the one person who can do it? Because of what I am?"

"You're only half-beast," he reminded her.

Aveline was quiet, considering. What if she could save Tiana and the rest of the city from her father? If Tiana was safe, then she could go to the Freelands, and Aveline's oath would be fulfilled. She did not want to part ways with her friend, but the two of them had two very different goals in life.

"Let's look at this logically," Rocky said. "Do a dry run. Go through the motions you would go through if you were serious about it. I guarantee you will walk away from him when you realize it's impossible."

"Smart. As always." Aveline lowered her deformed arm.

"Your father always said an assassination is successful here first." Rocky tapped his temple. "You have that look on your face. Promise me you will think about it before you do anything."

"I will," Aveline promised. "And if it seems impossible, I won't try."

Rocky appeared to accept her words, for which she was grateful. Deep down, she knew she had already made her decision to carry out her promise to Arthur and Tiana by protecting Tiana from the man Tiana feared most in the world.

Impossible or not, Aveline was going to find Karl and then kill Tiana's father – or die trying.

CHAPTER FOUR

TIANA'S DREAD AND FEAR had been building since the discussion earlier with Aveline, who believed they would be condemned to death or slavery by the council. By the time Tiana stepped into the hot tent to meet the tribal council later that night, she was overwhelmed and fighting back tears.

Eight women sat in positions of importance on a dais at the far end. What looked like half the village had crammed itself into the small space to watch the interviews, which had been going on all day long. The talk fell silent when she entered, Aveline at her side. Whether it was the charged energy of the tent, the heat that caused sweat to drip down her face before she reached her position standing in front of the council, or the stares, or a combination of all the sensations, Tiana was claustrophobic and felt sick to her stomach. The space in which she stood, before the council of middle aged and elderly women wearing severe expressions, was as confining as her old room. Her father had regarded her with this same expression every time they met. Disapproval, if not disgust, was clear on the faces of the women.

I cannot do this, she thought. *I cannot go back.*

Her only conscious thought was of returning to the hellish room, or worse – a cage, where she would spend the rest of her existence. Her ears began to ring, and her hair lifted wildly into the air around her.

"State your names," one of the women boomed.

Tiana's attention snapped to her. Aveline nudged her, and Tiana cleared her throat. "Tiana Hanover," she replied.

"Aveline Gerard."

Tiana sank into her mind and senses, unable to follow the discussion occurring on the dais when she was struggling to draw a deep enough breath. The women talked, Aveline responded, and murmurs went through the crowd. The pattern repeated itself, until silence fell.

Aveline nudged her again. "Say *yes*," she urged.

Tiana blinked and glanced from her friend to the council. She did as Aveline said, trusting her friend with her life. Her breathing grew shallower. When tunnel vision formed and the drink ware and other belongings of the council members began to lift into the air and spin, Tiana panicked.

She raced out of the tent, desperate for air and to feel the great outdoors. Tiana stumbled twice in the mud left over from a day of rain and continued onward, heading for the peace and quiet of the forest.

Tears stung her eyes and blurred her path. She ran until the terror she experienced whenever she thought of returning to her father released her. When nothing but the patter of rain against leaves filled her ears, and the cold water dripping down her face penetrated her frantic escape, she slowed and then stopped. Tiana sank down onto her knees and leaned against a tree. Her hands shook, and her mind would not focus on any one thing let alone clarify the fog surrounding what had been said by the tribal council.

She had not had a panic attack since leaving the city. Tiana waited for the vise around her chest to release its hold. She found herself gripping the small knife Red Moon had given her and pushed up her sleeve.

Slicing into her skin, Tiana released a breath. Pain penetrated her thoughts, giving them some cohesion among her chaotic emotions. Her hair, along with the loose branches and rocks in her surroundings, lowered and returned to their natural positions.

She sagged. Matilda had been wrong about bleeding out her magic, but the sensation of cutting her skin and the pain that followed always grounded her when nothing else seemed to.

Tiana cut the scarred skin of her inner arm again and relaxed further. Warm blood streamed down her arm and mixed with rain. She drew her first deep breath and lifted her face to the night sky. The rain was cold, the mud beneath her numbing her exposed skin, but she could imagine nowhere else she wanted to be. She dropped the knife and let herself dwell in the dull pain until she was shaking and soaked.

A pool of warm light lifted the gloomy night from the area around her. It was red light, not harsh enough to disturb her sensitive eyes yet bright enough to guide someone's path.

"Why are you bleeding?"

She tensed at Diving Eagle's terse voice. He was always angry with her or seemed ready to strike her. Tiana hunched her shoulders, waiting for him to hit her, now that they were alone and his father was not there to protect her. He crouched in front of her and gripped her injured arm, turning the soft skin of her forearm upward so he could assess the damage in the light.

Tiana twisted her arm away, but he held it tightly. "These are not animal bites or scratches from trees," he said.

"I did it," she whispered.

He glanced from her forearm to her face then back.

His normal disapproval was clear on his features, and he pulled out a small roll of bandages from the pouch at his waist.

Why would you do this to yourself? She read the question in his mind.

Tiana feared demonstrating another of her capabilities by answering. She watched him wrap her arm in a bandage. "Your father is not here. You do not have to pretend to tend to me," she said.

"My father taught me to do what I believed to be right for my people, no matter who is present to see it."

"My father taught me to suffer."

His hands paused. "You wish me to pity you?" His tone hardened.

"I speak only the truth," she replied. "You have a good father. I hope you cherish him."

"He is the most honorable man in the world." He continued with the bandage. "He is gifted. Like you."

"He is?" she asked, interested for the first time in anything this man had ever said to her. "What is his deformity?"

"It is not a deformity," was the curt response. "It is a blessing."

"Mine is not," she said quietly, distraught.

"No," he agreed. "Yours is not." He was quiet for a breath before he spoke again. "My father is a peacemaker. He has negotiated treaties and trade agreements with tribes who have been enemies of my people for hundreds of years. Every single one – except for the Hanover's."

"I have heard us called blood enemies," she said.

"We had several blood enemies at one time," he replied. "My father met your father once, twenty years ago." He dropped his hands and replaced the bandages in the pouch. "My father went with the intention of offering peace, because peace is the legacy he wanted to leave after our people have suffered through four and a half centuries of war. He looked into your father's eyes, and he left the meeting without speaking."

Tiana listened, fascinated by an account of her father she had never heard before. "Why? What happened?"

"My father's gift is the ability to see the spirit of everyone he meets. He can read intentions, and he knows when someone is good and when someone cannot be salvaged," Diving Eagle said. "When he saw your father, he saw a man with a spirit not of this world, born of evil so great, even my father declared that my people must always be at war with him and any Hanover who possessed this … thing inside him."

Tiana's pulse raced. She feared asking the question at the tip of her tongue. Diving Eagle was quiet, and at last, she whispered the words. "What did he see in Arthur and me?"

"Not that, or you would be dead," Diving Eagle replied. "He did not share with me what he saw, but he has defied everything we stood for to protect you." Diving Eagle gripped her arms and rose, lifting her with him. "He is never wrong, and I do not question him."

Tiana rested her palms against his warm chest to catch her balance and just as quickly snatched her hands back. He was close enough for her to smell his masculine scent. She braced herself and waited for him to leave.

Diving Eagle released her. "The council is debating whether or not to accept my father's decision. They understand his insight is unique, but the war between your family and mine extends centuries before any of us were born."

"Do you share his gift?" she asked. "Can you see my spirit?"

"If I could, I would not have invited a skinwalker into the midst of my warriors," he growled. "And I would not be indebted to a Hanover for saving them and my father."

"I was not trying to save your warriors," she said before she could stop herself. "I did not even kill the skinwalker like I wanted to." Reminded of this fact, she reached up and plucked the feather from her hair. "Red Moon said I earned this, but I did not." She handed it to him.

Diving Eagle accepted it with a glance. "Your intention is not in question. My failure to protect my people is. My father is the greatest chief since the Old World fell. His health is failing, but it is my judgment that almost ended his life."

That Diving Eagle experienced any emotion other than anger surprised her, and she ventured to look up into his features. "But it did not," she said. "You could not know what he was."

"I should have."

"No," she said. "You should not have. I saw him in a vision where he destroyed everyone I love. You do not have my deformity, for which you should be grateful. You will never have to flee your family and home because your father wants you dead, and you will never fear what you are, and what you might do if you are distressed or cornered, because you already know what you are capable of."

"Is that why you fled the council? Because you feared what you would do?"

"No. I felt … trapped. Like I did under my father's guardianship," she replied. "I want to be free. I cannot go back to being trapped. Ever."

"Free." He repeated the word as if trying to decide what it meant.

"I want to go to the Freelands and stay there forever."

"They may not exist."

"And if they do? No one can say with certainty they do not."

He shook his head and stepped away from her. "Your dream is foolish."

Tiana breathed deeply, relieved not to be confronted by his intensity any longer. He was not the first to call her desire this. Aveline and Arthur thought her foolish as well.

"I imagine it is better to be foolish and free than enslaved to your father," Diving Eagle added. "The council is debating your fate. You may return to the tent you share with the assassin." He waited.

Tiana looked around but could not identify which direction either of them had come from. She had run far enough for the smell of smoke and well-lit tents to be hidden by the forest.

"Come on," the Native warrior said. He turned and began walking.

She trailed him, shivering but grateful to be cold and wet and in the forest instead of confined with the council in the warm tent. She dared not ask what he thought the council would decide for fear of the answer.

Diving Eagle led her through the forest, back to the mobile village and left her at the tent without a word. Sensing them, Aveline shoved the tent door open.

"What were you thinking, Tiana?" she exclaimed and gripped her arm to tug her into the warm, cozy tent they shared. "Where did you go?"

Tiana was ready to cry when she noticed that the thick bear hair had crawled all the way up Aveline's neck and jaw and half her cheek. The image of Aveline with a beard made her smile instead.

Aveline rolled her eyes. "Change clothes. The council will decide at any moment what to do with us." She tossed clean clothes at Tiana. Her eyes lingered on Tiana's bandaged arm, but she said nothing about the self-inflicted wounds.

"I am sorry for leaving you, Aveline," Tiana said after she had changed. "I should have stayed. You might have been in danger. But I ..." She sighed.

"I can handle myself," Aveline said and then added. "I understand. I wanted to run, too. That was one hostile bunch of women."

"Do they trust their leader enough not to murder us?" Tiana joked weakly.

"The only thing clear to me is that they hate your family and everything you stand for," Aveline said and sat beside the cheerful fire at the center of the tent.

Tiana's heart sank. She silently berated herself for not being strong enough to conquer her fear and remain.

"But I have a feeling we are useful to them, and they know this," Aveline added. "They would be foolish not to use us, especially when we are willing to help."

"Did they mention Arthur?"

"Once, and I got the impression they know where he is but cannot get to him right now."

"Hopefully he can ..." Tiana trailed off. She did not know how to finish this thought or sentence. The Natives had been torturing her brother, and she had no desire for Arthur to return to their father. "Hopefully he is safe."

"Arthur has decent survival sense," Aveline said. "You both have been sheltered from the world, but I think he understands how to navigate people better than you do. He did not spend his life locked in a closet."

Tiana braided her wet hair and sat beside her friend. The brilliant glow of Aveline's pendant – a gift from the electrical engineer in the basement of the pyramid – made her glance down at the matching necklace she wore. Aveline was fidgeting, tugging at the hair of her bear arm. Tiana suspected her friend was not as thrilled by her new-formed deformity as Tiana had been.

"Are your friends okay?" she asked.

"For now," Aveline said, frowning. "I hope it stays that way. It'll probably depend on what the council decides." She shook her head. "Something weird is going on, Tiana. I mean … relatively weird." She lifted her bear claw. "The council seemed to think you are your father's heir, not Arthur."

Tiana laughed. "Never!"

"I know. But the way they talked about you was weird."

Tiana leaned back to grab a blanket and wrapped it around her shoulders. "My father hates that I am alive."

"I told them that. And told them their village wouldn't have been spared if not for you."

Tiana glanced at her friend at the mention of the incident in which she had tried to crush the skinwalker. "Do you think I'm evil, Aveline?" she asked quietly.

"You? No. There is not even an evil thought in your head."

"What about my deformity? Could it come from an evil source?"

Aveline gazed at her claw, features drawn. "I may be half-skinwalker, but I don't have the urge to wipe out villages like the full skinwalker did. I don't think our deformities are good or evil. I think *we* determine that. You could never be evil, not even a little, and I'm content being ignorant of whether or not an assassin would be considered evil."

Reassured by Aveline's confidence, Tiana began to relax. Diving Eagle would not agree, but Aveline knew her better. "I am happy we met, Aveline," she murmured and hugged herself.

"I am, too."

"And I like your bear claw."

"It's growing on me," Aveline said with less enthusiasm.

"Literally," Tiana said with a soft laugh.

Aveline pushed her away with a smile. "Go get some sleep. Whatever happens next will happen quickly."

Tiana rose and crossed to the bed she had claimed as hers. She lay down facing the fire and closed her eyes, happy Aveline was there to protect her.

Tiana's vision flared to life soon after her eyelids closed. It occurred in the same place she had witnessed the skinwalker brutally murder everyone she loved except this time, no one else was present aside from her and the skinwalker.

They stood in the quiet forest near the lodge she had yet to find in real life. He was unarmed and in human form, his lean frame supported by one natural leg and one that was clad in black. Behind him, spectral images of people she did not know milled. There were hundreds of them, perhaps thousands. The only one of them paying attention to her was a ghost boy around the age of ten with a slashed chest. This one stood close enough to listen to their discussion.

Tiana risked a look around her. Forest was on every side without any sign of anyone else who had been present previously.

"We have to do it," said the skinwalker.

"Pardon?" she asked, facing him again.

"No one else can."

"Do what?"

"Stop him."

"Tiana."

She snapped awake at Aveline's voice. The vision

remained, and Tiana sat and looked around to ensure they were safe. Light trickled in through the flap across the entrance, which had not been secured.

"It's time to go," Aveline said.

"Go where?" Tiana asked.

"You're going to find the skinwalker, and I am going on a mission."

Tiana's breath caught in her throat. "The council does not want us dead?"

"Not yet apparently." Aveline grunted as she pulled on her boots. "We're useful, as I hoped." She laced the second boot and stood. "Rocky's going with you."

"I had a vision about him," Tiana said thoughtfully.

"Rocky?"

"No, the skinwalker."

"Was he savagely murdering everyone again?"

"No." Tiana paused. "It was very different this time."

"Sounds like a good change to me," Aveline said with a distracted glance towards the entrance.

"I do not know for certain. The vision was too short."

"Listen, Tiana." Aveline's hushed voice drew Tiana's gaze. "I don't trust the Natives to be honest with us about our … *your* fate. They are sending me to the city. I'll be safe. I don't think you will be here."

Tiana frowned. She did not have Aveline's insight into people and had not suspected anything of those around her.

"Survive. Whatever it takes," Aveline told her. "Promise me you will do what you must."

"I will," Tiana said. "But you must promise to return to me."

Aveline hesitated. "I don't know that I can guarantee that, Tiana."

"Why not?"

"Because they want me to assassinate your father, and I don't know if I can." She flexed her bear claw.

Tiana sat in quiet surprise before she spoke again. "They want you to kill my father?"

"They think it'll allow them to attack the city."

"What about the people?" Tiana asked.

"What people?"

"There are tens of thousands of people in Lost Vegas."

Aveline shrugged. "Maybe they will take it over and replace him. It's not my concern."

It was rare when Tiana was dissatisfied with an answer someone gave her. "This sounds like a poor plan. All of it."

Aveline straightened. "I have no choice, and neither do you. We will both die if we don't cooperate, and they'll kill Jose and Rocky, too." Her grave warning silenced Tiana's concerns – for the time being. "If I don't return, stay with Rocky. Your father has survived assassination attempts his entire life by Guild members. I may not have much of a chance."

Tiana understood Aveline's point and chewed her lower lip, pensive.

"I have little time to plan. There must be some point where your father could be vulnerable. Can you think of anything?" Aveline asked.

Tiana sifted through what she knew of her father's routine. It was next to nothing, since she was rarely informed of his doings at all. "I do not know," she said, feeling worthless to help her friend. "Do not face him, Aveline. You do not understand the danger."

"I have no choice. He is the greatest threat to your safety, and I swore to protect you. This is me doing that job." Aveline pulled on a light coat of waterproofed leather and fleece lining. She started towards the door.

"Wait!" Tiana said, panic stirring within her. She threw her arms around her guardian in a bear hug.

Aveline sighed and reluctantly returned the hug.

"I can think of only one instance where I know anything of my father's schedule. Every Sunday night, my father goes into the secret passages," Tiana said.

"You know this how?"

"I heard him one night when I was waiting for Arthur to return. The passages used to lead somewhere, but were walled off. I heard someone moving through a passage on the other side of the wall in the part of the passage bordering my father's quarters. Matilda was asleep, and Arthur had not yet returned. It could only have been my father," she answered. "I listened every day for months, and it occurred every Sunday night."

"That might help." Aveline released her and pulled away. "I'll have to slip by the guards and return to your closet. Is there any other entrance to the passages in the walls?"

Tiana shook her head. "I searched for years to find a way out," she said sadly. "If there is, it must be in my father's quarters."

"Thanks, Tiana."

"You must come back, Aveline," Tiana said. The air around her became charged with energy stemming from her deformities, which responded to her unsettled emotion. No one, especially not her father, would hurt Aveline or anyone else she cared about ever again.

"I'll try." Aveline started towards the entrance again.

"You do not understand, Aveline," Tiana added. "If you do not return, I will come after you."

Aveline paused, her hand on the flap of the tent. "No, Tiana. You could never navigate the city on your own, and your father is too dangerous."

"So am I, Aveline," Tiana responded, thoughts on how easy it had been to fend off the Ghouls and skinwalker. "Or ... I can be."

"Whether or not I return, go be free in the Freelands. It's what you always wanted." Still frowning, Aveline flung open the tent flap and strode into the cool morning.

Not if you and Arthur die. Tiana did not have time to voice her words.

Troubled by Aveline's mission, Tiana was also surprised to find the depths of her own resolve when it came to saving those she cared about. Would she face her father?

The thought of standing up to him terrified her.

Recalling Aveline's news about the council's decision, Tiana dressed quickly and left the tent, anxious to hear what her role in tracking the skinwalker would be. Her vision replayed in her thoughts, and she debated what the skinwalker had been about to tell her before the dream ended. Had she changed the future by attacking him before he tried to hurt her friends?

The morning was cloudy but the rain had stopped. Rocky waited nearby, talking to the second man they had traveled with, Jose. A group of Natives – including Diving Eagle – mingled at the center of the village. They were dressed for travel with saddlebags and bedrolls slung over their shoulders.

Aveline approached her friends. She hugged Rocky and then walked a short distance away to speak to Jose in private.

Tiana hung back from everyone, feeling alone without Aveline. She gripped the pendant hard with one hand. If Aveline did not return, or if her father killed her friend, Tiana would use every last one of her deformities to find justice.

Diving Eagle left the group and approached her. Rocky moved towards her simultaneously and stopped beside her.

Tiana dropped her gaze to the ground and waited.

"We will leave as soon as the horses are brought to us," Diving Eagle informed them both.

"Can't wait," Rocky replied. "Let's go find us a skinwalker!"

Tiana peered at him from the corner of her eyes, curious. Around her brother's age, Rocky wore assassin blacks. His smile was quick for a trained killer, his dark eyes warm and sharp. While he appeared at ease, she picked up a similar subdued tension that Aveline possessed. Even when her friend relaxed, she was always ready to leap into action, and so was Rocky.

Diving Eagle appeared neither impressed nor irritated by Rocky's genuine enthusiasm. That he tolerated the assassin was probably the most pleasant he was capable of being with his enemies.

"My father asked me to give you this," the warrior continued and handed Tiana a pouch the size of her hand.

She accepted it without a word and waited for him to turn and leave before she opened it. Inside was the feather she had returned to Diving Eagle, along with a bracelet of turquoise beads, separated by wooden spacers carved in the shapes of animals. She smiled, touched by the gift from the man who had sought to protect her despite his hatred for her father. She slid the bracelet over her wrist but left the feather. Red Moon had told her only warriors who killed in battle were allowed to wear the feathers, and she had failed in her first battle with the skinwalker.

She tucked the pouch in her satchel.

Her second surprise of the day: Red Moon and other young men from the village brought them all mules instead of horses. The scrawny youth she befriended brought hers and Rocky to them with a smile. Her mule was chubby, smaller than the others, and furry with its winter coat.

"His name is Bear, because all he does is eat like a bear before hibernating," Red Moon told her.

"He is beautiful," she said and accepted the reins. "Are you coming with us?"

"Not this time. I'm staying here to help Father with a trade agreement," the youth said with confidence she had never held for anything in her life. "But I'll be here when you return with the skinwalker."

"Mount up!" Diving Eagle called.

"Thank you," she said to Red Moon.

Tiana mounted and saw Rocky do the same. They guided their horses to join the group of five accompanying them.

"We are headed north, where the last sign of the

skinwalker was found," Diving Eagle said. "I sent word to our neighbors not to engage him, if found, and to let us handle him."

"You mean let Tiana handle him," Rocky said with some amusement.

"She is the only one who can."

Not expecting Diving Eagle to agree, Tiana hid her smile. He was reluctant in his praise of her, even when everyone understood how ineffective normal weapons were. She guessed he remained angry with himself for not knowing about the skinwalker when he brought the creature into camp.

Diving Eagle trotted his horse to the front of the column to lead the search party into the forest.

"Funny how hard he tries not to admit what's in front of him," Rocky said for her ears only. "Stay close, Tiana. We're not safe here, no matter what they tell you."

"I have been treated well here," she replied.

"But have they told you what happens when you do what they want? When you become disposable?"

"They said I can go wherever I want."

"How? Do they intend to provide an escort? A map? Will they fund your journey? Because traveling that far will be expensive."

She studied him then looked towards Diving Eagle. "They said nothing about any of this," she said.

"When someone makes a promise but offers no

details, assume they are lying," he advised. "I know you can smash us faster than we smash flies in summer, but that power only works when you know to use it."

I see why Aveline trusts him, Tiana thought. Rocky possessed the same street and people sense as her friend. "I am ready," she told him.

"Good. Let's go catch us a monster." Rocky lifted his chin to motion her to follow the chain of warriors.

No sooner had the group begun to file out of the village than a rider on horseback barreled into the otherwise quiet area. Tiana heard his shout and glanced over her shoulder. His gaze swept past all of them and settled on Diving Eagle. The rider cantered down the line and stopped beside the chief's son.

Their procession stopped.

"I'd say that's bad news," Rocky said quietly from his position on the horse following hers.

Tiana studied the two at the head of the column, who spoke too quietly for anyone else to hear. Diving Eagle's face remained expressionless, but his jaw clenched. He gave a terse nod then waved the Native on the horse behind him to approach.

"Really bad news," Rocky added.

Tiana waited, trusting his instincts and taking note of Diving Eagle's mannerisms. He was difficult to read, more so considering she had rarely spoken to anyone before a few weeks ago. Their exchange the night before lingered in her mind.

There was more to him than anger. He cared for his people.

He did not seem like someone who could care for anyone at all, and this insight left her wondering if her own father – who had often wished her dead – might also care for her behind his cruel façade. He normally spoke out of anger or disappointment, but what if those emotions did not cloud his behavior when he dealt with her?

She had never thought him possible of anything more than what he displayed. If she were learning one thing about people, it was that there was more to them than she could possibly know.

The messenger left the head of the column to return to the village. After a moment of discussion, Diving Eagle turned his mule and walked down the line towards her. Rocky edged out around her horse to hear.

"We know where he is," he reported.

"Shortest hunt ever," Rocky said with a smile. "What's next?"

Diving Eagle shook his head, and his gaze grew distant for a moment. "It will be complicated."

"A large raid? Or do you need my assassin services for more discretion?"

"Neither. We are allied with the tribe who has him," Diving Eagle said. "You and I are going." This he directed to Tiana.

"Not alone," Rocky said instantly.

"If you insist." Diving Eagle addressed her still.

"I do," she said quietly.

"Then the three of us will go." He spun his horse and started off once more, this time not followed by the group of other Natives.

Tiana glanced at Rocky. He gave no indication he thought this was a bad idea. She squeezed her mule with her legs and followed Diving Eagle.

CHAPTER FIVE

ARTHUR SAT UP STRAIGHT before he was fully awake. His mind clung to the lucid dream that woke him, and the muscles of his body were tense enough to ache. He opened his eyes and blinked rapidly to ground himself from the vision.

He lay on one of the beds in the small medical clinic belonging to the Natives who reluctantly agreed to help him and Marshall. In the bed beside his was the skinwalker, who appeared to be swaddled from head to foot in linen bandages. Marshall lay sleeping in the row of beds across from him, while the she-wolf had stretched out on the floor between Arthur and the skinwalker.

Grainy, pre-dawn light filtered through the windows of the clinic. Arthur wiped his face, alarmed as much by the vision as by his heavy sleep.

"How long have I slept?" he asked the Native tending the skinwalker.

"A day and a half."

Arthur sighed. "Too long!"

"You were talking in your sleep. Nightmare?" the Native healer asked.

"I wish." Arthur shivered and twisted away to hide his face. He spotted the basket at the end of his bed and threw off the blankets carefully to avoid disturbing the pups sleeping within.

A nightmare would have been better than the vision lingering in his thoughts. Arthur had witnessed the city collapsing in on itself and being swallowed by the earth. In the middle of it all, standing on the edge of the abyss, watching it happen, was his father, who had left the city to find his children.

No Hanover had ever left the city once he became the leader. If this dream were the reason why, then Arthur would never again question this custom. He did not understand fully why this was the case, or why Lost Vegas had appeared to collapse the moment his father stepped outside.

The skinwalker had told Arthur the day before that the visions were exactly what they appeared to be. Unlike most of Arthur's visions, which appeared to have some room for interpretation, this vision did not. There was no second-guessing what he had seen.

Edwin Hanover had always said there were secrets to leading, and to the family history, he would pass down only upon his deathbed to his heir. Arthur had to believe the history of their deformities was one of these secrets but could not fathom what else his father hid. A secret powerful enough to destroy the city?

His mind worked fast, and he recalled the strange rumors the Natives believed about his father. He had always dismissed the strange talk of an unnatural army raised from the dead, or in some cases, an army of shadows that prevented any force from taking the city. He had viewed this talk as nonsense, the kind of tales told to children by their parents to scare them into behaving.

Until a few weeks ago, the skinwalker had been one of these tales.

"Are you hungry?" the healer asked.

Arthur shook his head and stood. "I have to leave."

"Your friend is not well enough to go with you," the Native said.

"That man is no friend of mine," Arthur said with a glance at the skinwalker.

"Not him." The healer pointed to one of the private rooms at one end of the small medical bay.

Not certain who he meant, Arthur nonetheless approached the door and pushed it open.

His breath caught in his throat, and his heart flipped over in his breast. "Warner!" he exclaimed and hurried forward. He dropped to his knees beside the low bed of his lover and friend and scoured Warner's features.

The dark-haired man was paler than usual, his skin clammy. He was unconscious. Warner's upper body was exposed, and a white bandage spotted with black wrapped around his body.

Arthur gripped Warner's calloused hand, thrilled to find his friend after weeks of wondering if he had survived the skinwalker attack. "I cannot believe you outsmarted that thing," he whispered proudly. "If anyone could defeat a skinwalker, it is you."

Warner was unresponsive to his voice, and Arthur's happiness shifted. He glanced again at the wound, frowning when he saw more black spots soak through the bandage. He touched one and lifted his hand, able to make out the combination of blood and black.

The skinwalker claimed it was a magic wound. The coloring was indeed unnatural.

"No salve or medicines will stop his bleeding," the healer said quietly. "It was always said that a wound inflicted by the skinwalker does not heal. I never believed it, until now."

Concern spun through Arthur. He had been hoping the skinwalker was lying about being the only person who could help Warner.

"He has been in this state since bringing his sister here."

"His … ahh." Arthur recalled Tiana's tale of pretending to be Warner's sister so no one knew she was a Hanover.

Arthur sat in silence, studying Warner's face. The sense of urgency, left over from his vision, fueled his blood with adrenaline, but he was having a hard time leaving Warner's side despite knowing the storm headed their way.

"I will waken your friend and bring you both breakfast," the healer said.

"No," Arthur said quickly. "I am leaving. Marshall will not like that, but he and Warner must remain here. Actually, all three of them must stay."

"You may wish to speak to Chases Deer before she leaves on her hunt. She was undecided what to do with all of you, the last time we spoke."

It took Arthur a moment to place the name of the Newe chief's daughter and heiress, a warrior said to possess the agility of an antelope. "Very well. May I have some clothing?" Arthur asked. "I do not wish to disrespect her dressed like this." He glanced down at the smelly, torn rags he had been wearing in a cage for several days.

The Native nodded and left the doorway.

"Hang in there, love," Arthur whispered to Warner. He leaned forward and kissed his lover's forehead. "I will return with a way to heal you."

He left the room, fidgeting and distressed to see his friend lying motionless in bed. The Native was out of sight in one of the rooms on the other end of the bay, and Arthur crossed to the wolf.

"Hey, wolf friend," he said and crouched beside her.

She cracked an eye open and wagged her tail. Her fur was a patchwork of black and white this morning.

"I need to leave. It is urgent," he said. "The others must stay here, but I am uncertain what their circumstances will become after I leave. Can you safeguard them? For a short time at least?"

She lifted her head, glanced towards the mangled body of the sleeping skinwalker, and snorted, as if to remind him she could go nowhere so long as her companion was hurt.

"We always end up with me in your debt," he observed. "One day, I will repay you for everything."

She dropped her head back to the wooden floor. Arthur lifted her basket of pups off the bed and placed them beside her then stood, gazing down at the skinwalker.

The only reason the Native was alive was because of the wolf. The tangled relationship among the three of them left Arthur frustrated and upset when he allowed himself to acknowledge how much damage was left in the skinwalker's wake – to include Warner's un-healing wound.

Why did the wolf choose to accompany the creature? From what Arthur had experienced, the wolf had compassion and an understanding of how to relate with humans, unlike the skinwalker she safeguarded. What benefit was there to her in their friendship? Why was a good spirit staying with a rotten one?

Worry about Warner, Marshall, and Tiana caused Arthur to fidget and then pace. The healer returned with clothing and an apple and handed them to Arthur.

"Thank you," he accepted the clothes and stripped off the rags he wore. Arthur's thoughts moved too fast for him to catch, and his hands fumbled with the clothing. He drew a deep breath, aware both the wolf and healer were watching him, and then tried again to tug on his clothing.

"You should wait to leave until the doves come," the healer said.

"Doves?" Arthur echoed, his voice muffled by the shirt he pulled on.

"Every day, your father sends out a hundred doves carrying his demands."

Arthur cursed his father silently. Too mad to understand how many ways he had placed his children in danger, Edwin had long since destroyed the respect any Native in the vicinity of the city would otherwise have for the leader of the city. Arthur finished dressing.

"Where are these messages?" he asked.

"Chases Deer."

"Very well. I will stop to pay my respects and read my father's demands before I leave." Arthur smiled. "Thank you for tending to us despite my father."

The Native returned the smile. "You always bring us meat during the annual hunts. We do not do this for your father," he said.

Arthur nodded, suspecting as much. "I will bring you more than meat when I return," he promised. He did not need directions. He had come to this very village more than once over the years since he began leading the annual Winter Hunt.

Arthur stepped out into the cool morning and strode through the village, past the oldest tree in the forest, bedecked in lights, and into the permanent part of the village. During late winter, when hunting parties returned to this area to hunt, the village swelled to three times its size. The semi-permanent tents along two sides of the village marked the presence of the hunting parties, while the more permanent family homes were tucked deeper into the forest.

The chief's ambassador to the village during the hunt was a trim woman Arthur had met on two occasions. One of the rare female warriors, she was revered for her agility and ferocity in battle.

Arthur navigated the quiet village, eyes roving each home he passed for the familiar mark of the chief: a hawk carrying a feather. He found the pennant pinned outside the home he sought and knocked at the door.

Chases Deer opened the door fully dressed, down to her boots, and carrying a warrior's weapons: a rifle and knives. She was his height with dark hair and eyes and a birthmark on one cheek.

"I apologize for disturbing you so early," Arthur said.

"You do not disturb me," she replied. "We are riding out early today to search for elephants."

"Really?" His eyebrows lifted. "What is the occasion?" Elephants, rare in this part of the country, were prized by the Natives of some tribes and viewed as signs of stature and luck.

"My father believes he has married me off," she replied somewhat tartly.

"Ah." Arthur smiled. "I know that pain. My father has tried on more than one occasion to marry me off as well. It is the curse of the firstborn, is it not?"

"A great curse," she agreed. "Come, Hanover." She pushed the door open wider and stepped back.

"I wanted to thank you for your hospitality before I left," he said and walked into her lodging. "And ask another favor."

"Have I not done enough for you?" she challenged.

"More than enough. But this will benefit us both, I believe."

"Go on."

"Keep my companions here until I return."

"If the Cruise heir is as rich as he claims, then I am happy to ransom him to you," she said with the cunning Arthur remembered.

"He is, and I am happy to pay the ransom for him and my injured companion, Warner. Just please do not put them in a cage," Arthur replied wryly. "We have had enough of cages for a lifetime."

"We do not share our neighbors' fervor with interrogation and torture. The Diné have developed a reputation for their conduct in battle. The promise of coin and goods are all I require," she said and crossed to collect two canteens and a satchel. "I thought you would ask for assistance ransoming your sister back from your enemies."

Arthur was quiet for a moment. If not for his vision, he would jump at the chance to work with Chases Deer to help his sister. As it was shaping up to be, Tiana was safer outside the city, in the hands of their traditional enemies, than she would ever be within reach of their father. "Perhaps when I return," he said slowly. "Does everyone know of the state of Hanover affairs?"

"That your father blames the Natives for kidnapping his children and is threatening war with every tribe between the city and ocean?"

"Is that what he claims?" Arthur could not account for his father's increasingly erratic behavior. While true,

Chases Deer's father was a longtime ally, Edwin Hanover was recklessly risking losing the cooperation of the very tribes with whom the city shared a symbiotic relationship. The city was not an island, as much as Edwin tried to make it one. The citizens of inner and outer cities depended upon the trading partnerships between city and Natives for basic staples.

Arthur was beginning to find it more difficult to overlook, or ignore, his father's negative impact on the world around them.

"I have no explanation for you," he said pensively. "I don't understand my fathers motivations anymore."

Chases Deer studied him for a long moment. "You are not like the other Hanover's."

"I should hope not." Arthur opened his mouth to point out how his grandfather and great grandfather had been different but stopped himself.

No ruling Hanover had ever possessed his right mind, not according to what Arthur knew of his predecessors.

"But you cower in your father's shadow," Chases Deer pointed out.

"Do we all not do the same?" he challenged softly.

She rolled her eyes at him in irritation. "My father asked me to explain how you were permitted not only to live, but to escape the Diné."

Arthur forced a laugh. "I cannot explain it myself," he admitted. "Diving Eagle wanted me dead, but his father intervened."

"It is not like Elk Hunter to pardon his blood enemy, and definitely not characteristic for Diving Eagle to spare anyone who displeases him."

"I understood that about him, too," Arthur said and touched his bruised eye.

"Yet you lived."

"We did."

She waited for more.

He shrugged. "I am not hiding anything from you, Chases Deer," he said. "I am not in a position to defy you when the lives of my friends are in your hands. I cannot explain why I was spared any more than I can explain my father's actions of late."

Her hard features softened. "You are lost."

"I am."

She glanced towards the door, as if concerned someone would interfere, then moved closer to him and lowered her voice. "My own father wants to free you as well, against my wishes."

"I am grateful to you and your father," Arthur said with eloquence that would impress even Marshall.

She snorted.

"I understand what the Hanover heir is worth," he added. "I have nothing of value to barter with you, and no weapons to fight you. All I can do is give you my word I will do all I can to spare your people the wrath of my father."

Chases Deer was quiet for a moment. "I do not know what tales to believe about your father, or why every Native chief fears him. Is he not a man like you?"

Not exactly, Arthur answered silently. Sensing there was no safe response, he waited for her decision.

"Your father's messages are over there. You may view them, if you do not already know what lies he tells, and then you will leave before any other tribe finds out you are here." She pointed to a trunk. "I will even give you my fastest horse to ensure you make it to the city. I cannot promise you that my people will not track you and capture you for ransom, but you are fortunate that I chose today of all days for my elephant hunt."

"The alliances are shifting," Arthur observed and went to the small wooden trunk. "Are we still allies at all?"

"We were never allies," she returned.

"Then why did my father favor your people?"

"Favor!" she snapped. "Threatening us every time the wind changes is not favoring us!"

"You never hesitated to trade with us."

"We had no choice," she allowed. "Lost Vegas is known even among the Natives for its metal workers and luxury goods, the benefit of controlling all trade on this side of the country. Your father's focus has always been on the city. He charges his allies a tenth the price it costs for him to import many of the rarer goods your city is known for. Spices from afar, silk, ore. His threats towards us have been hollow, and he never followed through with any of them as long as we respected the treaties. You being here has turned his focus to us, and no one is pleased, least of all my father, whose fears run too deep for me to believe they are without merit. The Hanover chief has already broken two trade agreements in the past week."

How did his father come to this point? How could anyone in their right mind believe angering the Natives surrounding the city was a good idea? Arthur hated that he could not explain his father's decisions, but he hated even more that he agreed with the Natives for being angry.

"So you are setting aside differences with the other tribes in preparation for war," Arthur guessed.

"Hence the marriage I do not want to Elk Hunter's barbarian son."

"Historically there is no better way to cement an alliance than ..."

Her glare made him pause. He could almost hear Marshall chiding him for not being diplomatic enough.

"Firstborn curse," he finished. "My apologies, if the arrangement is not to your liking."

"It is not," she said. She released a deep breath, and tension left her tall frame. "I prefer my situation to yours.

I know where I stand in all this."

Arthur smiled faintly.

"You have a respected reputation among my people and many others. For this reason, and because I am not yet ready to face your father, I will grant your request to treat your friends as guests rather than prisoners. Leave my village before I ransom you," she ordered quietly. "I'll give you til noon then send my youngest trackers after you." She stuffed the canteens and more weapons into the satchel before slinging on the satchel with agitated movements.

"Thank you," Arthur murmured and picked up the stack of thin strips of paper.

She did not reply but slammed open the door and walked out.

Arthur sat next to a light and began to read. True to his father's ways, the messages were each one sentence long and abrupt.

"Hanover."

He looked up at Chases Deer's voice.

She leaned through the doorway. "We do not want war," she told him. "But we will stop your father, or anyone, from hurting our people, by any means necessary."

"I understand," he responded. "I hope to stop whatever it is we all sense coming before it happens."

"I hope you can." She ducked outside once more.

"I do, too," Arthur whispered. Chases Deer could not know what he had seen in a vision, that nothing would stop the destruction his father would inflict, if Arthur did not act.

He started to read the earliest messages – dated two weeks ago, before Tiana's journey to the forest. Edwin Hanover had demanded the return of his heir multiple times. He offered no incentives for his allies to comply, only sent stark threats.

Use all your resources to see that my heir is returned, or I will use all of mine to punish you for failing me.

Each message became more difficult to read, not because Arthur was surprised but because he began to sense something in his father he had never noticed before: desperation. It left him uncomfortable. Edwin Hanover was never desperate, because he knew what power and influence he possessed at his fingertips. Arrogance was a truer representation of him.

Why would his father be desperate about anything?

Arthur skimmed several more messages before coming to one that jarred him out of his train of thought.

Negotiate the return of my daughter, and I will offer my son in marriage to your valiant daughter to celebrate our alliance.

Arthur uttered a low curse in surprise.

He re-read the politer note and checked the date then compared the handwriting to that of the other missives.

His father, who had refused to allow Arthur to attend routine council meetings in case an assassin caught them both in the same place, was offering him up to the Newe in exchange for Tiana.

Arthur read through the messages from the past few days with a sense of disbelief, if not outright confusion. Edwin had sent out two-dozen messages in three days, as opposed to the six messages sent out over the course of the two weeks preceding Tiana's escape from the city.

Every one of the dozen was about Tiana. None of them mentioned him, except to repeat the first concession of a marriage between the city and Natives to cement a truce.

"What is going on?" Arthur muttered aloud.

Why was Edwin willing to sacrifice his heir in exchange for the unwanted daughter who would not have survived her childhood, if not for Arthur?

"Hanover," someone called from outside the cabin.

Arthur remained in place for a moment, contemplating what was before him with little comprehension. Nothing made sense anymore. Not the skinwalker and his wolf, not Arthur's growing respect for a Cruise, not Tiana's emerging powers, not Edwin

Hanover. Arthur had the sense he had stepped into a new reality, one he was unprepared to deal with.

Finally, Arthur plucked the first message about Tiana free from the pile, replaced the rest of the messages, and rose. He strode to the door. One of the adolescent warriors in training held the reins to a gray horse.

"She did not jest about giving me her best horse," he said with a nod of appreciation. The stallion was one of the prized horses from Chases Deer's father's infamous band of rare Arabians. No finer animals were found for two thousand miles, and no other horse matched the stamina of his horses. The horse was saddled, bridled and bearing saddlebags with canteens dripping with water clipped to them.

The youth held out a handgun, two knives, and a pouch whose clicking sounds from within were those of flint.

"Much obliged," Arthur said and accepted the offerings. "Assure your warrior princess I will return when it benefits us both." *And not to marry her.* Although, this part he kept quiet. His heart belonged to the man sleeping in the clinic. He had managed to outmaneuver his father's attempts to marry him off for several years.

With the sun soon to break the horizon, Arthur dared not linger much longer. As unsettled as he was about abandoning Warner and Marshall to the kindness of allies who were quietly choosing a different side, he could not quell the urgency in his blood warning him something much worse awaited them all, if he did not reach the city before the scene from his vision unfolded and condemned everyone.

He mounted. The gray stallion pranced impatiently beneath him and tossed its head, eager to move.

Arthur did not dissuade him. They were both anxious.

With a nod at the youth, and one last glance in the direction of the clinic, he released his hold on the horse's head and urged him forward, towards the plains separating the village from the city.

Arthur reached the edge of the forest by noon. The roads through Native land coalesced into one solitary path leading towards the city. It was a matter of defense for the city, and an agreement made with the neighboring tribes, that only one road would be maintained in each cardinal direction.

Taking the road made Arthur a target.

Going around it extended his trip.

On any other horse, he would have chosen the slow route so he could hide if the Natives tracking him caught up. But on the fastest horse north of the city, Arthur brazenly chose to ride exposed and fast, straight for Lost Vegas.

CHAPTER SIX

HIS BACK TO HER AND eyes on the forest across the clearing, Diving Eagle tossed an apple in the air above his head. Tiana followed it with her eyes from her position seated at the base of a large tree. Rocky was moving through what he called fighting forms – smooth, controlled, slow blocks and strikes. He was sweating despite the cool mid-morning.

After a day of waiting in this spot for the neighboring Newe tribe to grant them permission to enter their territory, Tiana was bored enough to be antsy. Diving Eagle's rhythmic tossing of the apple provided her some distraction, though nothing seemed to take the edge off she had felt since she faced the skinwalker the first time.

Was his proximity the reason she was barely able to sit still? That the forest felt too small?

She absently ordered the apple to stay in the air without expecting it to obey.

But it did.

Tiana sat forward. She had never considered using her magic to occupy herself, not after a lifetime of being punished for failing to control it. Out here, with a man who disapproved of everything she did no matter what, and Rocky, who was not fazed by anything, she felt somewhat safe experimenting with it.

She tilted her head and ordered the apple to move in midair until it was over Diving Eagle's head. Then she let it fall again.

He was tense enough to jerk when the fruit hit his head. The Native warrior leaned forward to swipe the apple off the ground. He tossed it up again.

She shifted it midair and dropped it.

This time, he stared down at the apple on the ground, then glanced at his hand, before he plucked the fruit up again.

Tiana grinned.

He tossed it once more.

She did it again and dropped the apple on his head.

He turned to face her.

Tiana ducked her gaze but did not hide her smile before he saw it. She waited for him to reprimand her.

"You have some control over it?" he asked instead.

"I seem to," she replied.

He stepped back and grabbed the apple. "Do it again." He tossed it up over his head.

She paused it in midair.

Diving Eagle studied it. "Send it higher."

She obeyed.

"Send it across the field and back."

Tiana did.

He shook his head. "It requires no effort for you to do this?"

"Not this," she replied. "Facing the skinwalker drained me."

"But …"

She gazed at him blankly.

"You have additional insight."

She did. Not certain how he knew she had not completed her sentence, she nodded. "He … drained me. Or tried. What I experienced was not natural. When I was close to him, I felt recharged, until he starting pulling my ability from me."

"What part of that was your uncontrolled emotion?"

Tiana's cheeks flushed hot. The way he asked the question left her no doubt about what this careful man thought of *uncontrolled emotion.* "Most of it maybe," she mumbled.

He held out his hand, and she dropped the apple into it. "The more you practice, the better you will manage it when you are not in control," he advised. "You can be more than a weapon who throws skinwalkers into the sky."

Her brow furrowed. She had never considered *how* to use her abilities.

"I imagine you could build a village with your mind in a day," he continued. "Or herd enough buffalo for a tribe to live off of for the winter."

"There are practical uses for your talents," Rocky added, settling onto the ground beside her. "What exactly is the extent of your gift?"

Both of them gazed at her, waiting with an edge she was unable to interpret, but which left the hair on the back of her neck standing on end.

Were two of the bravest people she had ever met ... afraid? Of *her*?

How was that possible?

"I do not know," she admitted.

"We know you have crushed and thrown a skinwalker so far into the air, he landed five miles away," Rocky said. "And Aveline said you killed your stepmother by smashing her head."

Tiana's hands twisted in her lap. There was no judgment in his tone, and Diving Eagle appeared interested.

"You can levitate things with your mind and control them in the air," Rocky continued. "What else?"

"I ... well, I do not know how, but I made the Ghouls

leave us alone once," she said. "And I have visions of the future. Bad ones. This is how I recognized the skinwalker when I had never seen him before." She paused, thoughts on the latest vision, where the skinwalker had tried to speak to her rather than attack her. Tiana shook her head. "I also hear thoughts sometimes. Not often, though."

Her words were met with a long silence.

"You all have a word for this?" Rocky joked uneasily to Diving Eagle.

"No."

"My father calls them deformities," she said. "My brother has them as well."

"Does your father?" Rocky asked.

"Yes," Diving Eagle replied.

"No," she said simultaneously.

"I have a feeling he does," Rocky said. "It would explain how no one will oppose him after burning half the population of the city."

"I would prefer never to find out why he does what he does," she said softly. "I intend to never see him again."

"I wish you luck. It's rare when someone can escape his past." The wise words were quiet.

She glanced up at him, realizing she knew nothing of his story, either. She knew little of the men with her, especially how they thought or who they really were.

"Out of curiosity, how often do you read minds?" Rocky asked.

"Rarely," she replied. "Before last night, it had been weeks. I hear only a sentence or two."

"Last night?" Diving Eagle prodded. "Was this why you fled the council?"

"No. I read your mind."

He stared at her. Hard.

Rocky laughed. "A word of advice, Tiana. Don't tell people you can read their minds," he said. "Unless they're friends. Aveline and I wouldn't care, but some people might."

"Agreed," Diving Eagle and shifted to see the forest across the clearing once more.

Tiana sensed she had offended him. Rocky's wink and amused smile, however, left her feeling less concerned. If the assassin was not worried, she would not be, either.

The three settled into quiet again. Diving Eagle replaced the apple in his bag and walked a few feet into the clearing.

Rocky removed two bone knives and began to polish them.

Tiana rested against the tree trunk and let her head fall back. The pine needles lining the branches above her head brought a smile to her face. Their rich scent and color were magical – and more beautiful than she ever imagined possible when she was trapped in her room in the city.

Her eyes drifted closed, and she drew several deep

breaths to help her wired body relax. She listened to the breeze whisper through the trees. The morning was the epitome of spring: cool air, warm sunshine, and filled with the bright songs of birds. An instinct stirred at the far reaches of her mind, almost too faint and far for her to make out.

She opened her eyes and listened hard at what her deformities were trying to tell her. She was able to find someone with her mind when she actively tried. She had never experienced this sense before, though, as if someone was entering her mind unbidden to tell her he or she was present.

"I think someone is coming," she said and stood.

"I see no one," Diving Eagle said, eyes trained across the meadow.

Tiana listened again then faced to the right. "From that direction." She pointed to the east rather than the north.

Diving Eagle glanced from her to the trees. He appeared to think for a split second before starting off in the direction. "Wait here," he ordered them both.

Rocky swiftly returned his weapons to their sheaths at his waist and ankles then stood. "Can you make a tree fall on him?" he asked when Diving Eagle had disappeared into the forest.

Tiana looked at him in surprise.

"Not now," Rocky said quickly. "But in case he ends

up betraying you, like I think he will. Can you do that?"

"Probably," she replied.

"You're almost confident. That's an improvement," he said. "Remember – you always have the upper hand with us normal people. You can crush us at any time."

She absorbed the words, uncertain why they struck her as odd. "I would not purposely hurt anyone," she said.

"But you *can*. That's the important part. You should never feel scared of anyone or anything. You can take care of yourself."

"Except when I am not certain of the threat."

"That's what I'm for. To make sure no one gets to you before you crush them."

I do not plan to crush anyone ever, she said to herself. Tiana smiled faintly. She was starting to like Rocky as much as she had Aveline. For assassins, the pair were honest and helpful in a way no one else was.

They waited in comfortable silence.

Twenty minutes later, Diving Eagle reappeared, accompanied by a lean woman his height who was armed with more weapons than he, and four additional Natives trailing them.

Rocky's wariness increased. He shifted to a position ahead of Tiana by inches. Her eyes were on the warrior woman, who moved with the same controlled, efficient movement as the male warriors.

She and Diving Eagle walked abreast – but with

enough tension between them, even Tiana picked up that something was not right.

The warrior woman slowed as she approached, her eyes on Tiana. Diving Eagle joined Tiana and Rocky, staying a few feet in front of both.

The warrior woman looked from Tiana to Diving Eagle and spoke a flurry of words in her Native tongue.

"Speak so they can understand," Diving Eagle replied.

"This girl? Has she any muscles at all?" the woman said.

Diving Eagle's quiet rebuke was in his tongue.

"Respectful of what?" the woman retorted. "You demand access to *my* territory and *my* village and offer up a tale about a monster who will slaughter us all in our beds if I do not allow a girl without muscles into my village?"

"I act in your benefit," Diving Eagle replied. "It is out of respect for you and your father that I did not raid your village and take him. I would have raided any other tribe but I chose not to offend yours."

"If you took one step into my village uninvited, my father and his allies would crush you."

"Your father currently favors my tribe, because he understands what we have to offer."

"My father thinks you are a barbarian!" she snapped.

Diving Eagle turned away and sighed.

Tiana and Rocky exchanged a look.

"They are unhappy with one another, are they not?" she ventured.

"I'd say so. Might be time to make something float," Rocky advised.

Tiana had been thinking along the same lines. With Rocky's support, she focused on the angry warrior woman.

The Native lifted off the ground. Tiana concentrated, not wanting to hurt her, and gently lifted the woman into the air until she was a solid twenty feet up.

The Native woman had gone completely still and silent.

"If I were you, I would listen to Diving Eagle," Rocky called up to her. "There is a real threat in your village, and only this girl with no muscles can stop it before it hurts anyone else."

The female warrior erupted into what Tiana imagined were curses in her language. She thrashed in the air.

For once, Diving Eagle was smiling. Rather, half-smiling. Tiana doubted he was capable of a full smile, but the right side of his mouth tilted up as he watched the woman flailing above their heads.

Tiana lowered the woman to the ground. The Native stood very still for a moment and then released her breath. Her eyes settled on Tiana.

"You did that?" she demanded.

Tiana nodded.

After a thoughtful quiet, the warrior woman spun. "You may enter my village. You will be gone by dusk."

Rocky waited until she was a safe distance away before leaving to gather the horses.

"Why do you two hate one another?" Tiana asked Diving Eagle.

"Many reasons," was his curt response.

"Are we safe in her village?"

"Does it matter? You can throw her warriors into the forest."

Tiana said nothing. She had the sense those around her gave her more credit than she deserved. Lifting one woman into the air, and controlling her abilities when she was emotionally upset, were two separate skills. If someone attacked her, she was more likely to cry and run than fight.

They mounted their mules and trailed the warrior woman into a familiar village. Tiana cheered up when she recognized the place she had been before recently, on her way to find Arthur. They passed the tallest, oldest tree in the forest, whose lights were dark this day, and continued to the medical clinic at the center of the village.

Tiana dismounted before anyone else, eager to see if Warner had healed.

"Tiana!" Rocky called as she entered the wooden clinic unescorted.

She allowed her eyes to adjust for a split second. The

beds were empty, and she frowned, stepping deeper into the clinic. In one of the rooms off the main bay, she saw movement through a half open door and drew nearer.

A healer was changing the bandages on an unconscious Warner. He straightened when she pushed the door open.

"You return," he observed. "Your brother is no better."

She went to stand beside Warner. The black wound looked the same as the last time she had seen it. "He is not healing at all?" she asked, disturbed.

"His condition worsens."

Tiana knelt beside the low bed and rested a hand on Warner's warm skin. Her gifts were too vast for her to understand their limits. Was it possible for her to heal someone, too?

She concentrated and pushed the agitated magic towards Warner. His body glowed briefly before the energy sank into him. She kept her eyes pinned on the wound for signs it was healing.

It did not change.

She tried again, ignoring the presence of Rocky in the doorway.

No change.

Tiana dropped her arm. "I have limits," she reported to Rocky. "I cannot heal."

"No one is perfect," he said. "Who is this?"

"Warner. He traveled with me from the city."

Voices from the bay drew both of their attention. Tiana left Warner to join Rocky in the doorway.

Diving Eagle and the warrior woman were quietly arguing. The Native woman gesticulated towards a bed with rumpled bedding.

"Was someone else here?" Rocky asked the healer.

"A man with wounds that should have killed him," the healer said. "His body was crushed. He was barely breathing when they brought him in two evenings ago. This morning, he stood up and said he was well and walked out. I told him he could not leave the village. He said he would go where he pleased and vanished before my eyes. I have never seen anything like it."

Tiana's breath caught in her throat. She and Rocky looked at one another.

"That's not good," Rocky said for both of them.

"His companion has been placed under guard until the ransom promised by Arthur Hanover is paid," the healer added.

"Arthur was here?" Tiana asked.

"For the night. He left yesterday morning. His companions, and your brother, are being held for ransom."

"Brother?" Rocky asked with a glance at Warner. "You have two?"

"I have one," Tiana clarified. "But we thought it best

not to tell people who I was when I traveled, because everyone hates my father. Warner is a friend to Arthur."

"You're a Hanover," the healer said.

She nodded.

"Chases Deer knows where your brother went." The healer nodded towards the Native woman.

"She's a real warrior?" Rocky asked.

"The swiftest for a thousand miles. She will lead our people when her father dies, which many believe will be soon, because of his age," the healer answered.

"Amazing." Rocky's eyes glowed.

Tiana lifted an eyebrow at him.

"Not that her father will die," Rocky said quickly. "But a warrior princess. Aveline is the only female assassin in the city. She would love to hear this."

Tiana was not as certain. Chases Deer seemed much more confrontational than Aveline had ever been. She waited until there was a lull in the conversation between Diving Eagle and Chases Deer.

"If I may interrupt," she said, moving closer to the two. "The healer said my brother left yesterday morning. Do you know where he went?"

Chases Deer turned her intense gaze on Tiana. "Brother," she repeated.

"Arthur."

"You brought a Hanover into my village," Chases Deer said icily to Diving Eagle. "*The* Hanover everyone is looking for." She pushed past him and glanced at Tiana. "Your brother went to the city to stop your father from creating war with the Natives. You all will remain here until I have had a chance to speak to my father." She swept out of the clinic.

Only when she was gone did Diving Eagle roll his shoulders back and relax.

"You should have raided her village," Rocky said wisely.

"Agreed," the warrior seconded.

"I like her," Tiana said. Chases Deer did not fear Diving Eagle the way Tiana did. In fact, Tiana guessed the Native warrior feared no one for any reason.

I want to be like her. But she doubted she ever would, not when she feared herself as well as the rest of the world.

"We are stuck here for now?" Rocky asked their companion.

"It would seem so." Diving Eagle faced Tiana. "Can you sense the skinwalker?"

She tilted her head, listening and feeling for any kind of anomaly that might indicate the skinwalker was close. He had a definite impact on her; if he were nearby, she should know.

She left the confinement of the building and stood in the open space in front of it. Tiana closed her eyes. A tiny whirlwind of energy tossed her hair around her shoulders and lifted the loose layers of clothing she wore.

A whisper of an instinct came from one direction. She opened her eyes. Her clothing and hair settled once more.

"Maybe ..." she said and pointed to the west. It was too faint to determine with certainty, as if he were trying to hide himself from her. She turned to find Rocky and Diving Eagle regarding her with different levels of wariness on their features. Rocky managed to smile. Uncertain what had disturbed them, Tiana cleared her throat.

"The healer said your brother traveled with a companion." Rocky was the first to speak.

"Marshall," Diving Eagle supplied. "They both disappeared from our captivity."

"Marshall," Tiana repeated, recalling Marshall's sister Matilda, whom Tiana had accidentally killed. Little had she known Matilda would be the first of many Cruise deaths.

"Chases Deer said the spirit wolf is with him. The wolf is the skinwalker's companion. Perhaps she can take us to him."

Tiana was quiet. She did not want to face Marshall, a stranger she had met on only one other occasional before finding him and her brother chained in cages in Diving Eagle's village.

"Can you find Marshall?" Rocky asked her.

She shook her head. She did not wish to try.

"I may know where he is," Diving Eagle said and struck off in the direction of the large tree.

"You've been imprisoned here before?" Rocky and fell into step beside him.

"More than once."

Rocky laughed.

Tiana trailed, spirits dampened when she thought of Marshall and his family. He would hate her – for good reason. Disheartened to face another victim of her father's madness, she kept her thoughts to herself as she followed them through the village and to a small cabin guarded by two Natives.

They were permitted to pass through and entered. Tiana lingered in the doorway, afraid of Marshall's reaction. The wolf with marbled fur curled up on a blanket in the living area drew her attention. The last time she had seen it, the wolf was black.

"Marshall?" Rocky called.

"In here," came a voice from one of the rooms off the main living area.

The two men went towards Marshall, but Tiana crossed to the wolf instead. She knelt.

The great wolf lifted its head to peer at her with golden eyes.

Tiana reached out to it and ran her fingers through its hair. "What happened to you?" she whispered.

An image of six puppies flashed across her mind.

"Ah. Are they healthy?"

Yes.

"But you are not." Tiana touched the white fur. It was unnaturally cold compared to the black fur.

Dying.

Her fingers stilled. "I am so sorry. Why?"

My time.

"It is not because of a Hanover?" Tiana joked.

Hanover kind.

"You are the only one who thinks so."

Hanover good. Help others.

"I do not. My brother might but … I have been pretty useless," Tiana said. "Thank you, though, for the kind words."

"This is what I was telling you." Marshall's voice jarred her.

Tiana twisted, terrified to see him with a weapon ready to strike her down in revenge for murdering his sister. He stood several feet away, arms crossed, Rocky and Diving Eagle beside her.

He does not know.

Tiana glanced at the wolf.

Marshall good. Safe. Arthur scared to hurt him.

Tiana almost sighed. She had never heard of a *good* Cruise, but she knew nothing of the family outside of her experience with Matilda and what Arthur had shared with her.

"The Hanover's have this disconcerting ability to speak to magic wolves," Marshall said. "Do you not?"

It took Tiana a second to register his question. She was trying too hard not to imagine what it would be like if she lost her brother and everyone else she cared about.

Marshall did not know.

Should she tell him?

Yes, said the wolf.

"Yes," Tiana answered Marshall. "I can. She says she is dying."

"Does she speak of her master? The skinwalker?"

Tiana returned her attention to the wolf.

The image in her mind was a blur of forest and sky.

"I do not understand," she said.

You find him soon.

"She says we will find him soon," Tiana told the others.

They were quiet.

The wolf rested her head on her paws and closed her eyes. Tiana rubbed her ears, saddened by the idea of the animal dying. "Where are her puppies?" she asked.

"In my room," Marshall answered.

Truth. The wolf said quietly into Tiana's mind.

Tiana drew a deep breath. She stood and faced them. "Marshall, I need to speak to you."

"Speak," he replied curtly.

"Alone." She gave Rocky a look.

He nodded and stepped aside.

"Very well," Marshall looked between her and Rocky. "Come meet the puppies and we can talk."

She trailed him into his room and closed the door behind her. On his bed were six small puppies sleeping and surrounded by a blanket wall to prevent them from wandering off the bed.

"Supposedly, one of them is magic," Marshall said and knelt beside the narrow bed. "Your brother abandoned me here to the Natives."

"I am certain he had his reasons," she murmured.

"As am I. But he could have shared them with me. We have spent the last few weeks together in a wild chase to save *you* from a skinwalker whose life you almost took."

Tiana listened. She leaned over to peer at the puppies and smiled.

"I am ready to leave the forest behind and feast at your father's table again," Marshall added.

Her gaze rose, and she straightened. "That cannot happen, Marshall."

"Why not? I helped save your father's two stray dog children," he replied with no heat. "I feel I've earned my place at my father's side at the head table. Arthur and I put aside our differences. I would consider us friends."

Tiana's mouth felt dry. She wet her lips and drew a breath. How would Aveline broach the news to someone? Her assassin friend, much more experienced in the world, had always been direct with her.

"Marshall, your family is dead," Tiana said. "All of them."

He stared at her.

Tiana took a step back towards the door. "Arthur did not know," she added, wanting to spare her brother the dishonor of lying to a friend, Cruise or otherwise. "My father burned everyone."

Disbelief crossed Marshall's features. His mouth dropped open as he gazed at her. His cheeks flushed red. After a moment of shock, a strange sound emanated from his mouth, one that sounded half like a scream, half like a shout.

And then his hands were around her neck, and he was slamming her into the floor. Black edged Tiana's mind. She did not fight him and closed her eyes, preparing for a beating the likes of which his sister used to give her routinely.

The door slammed open. Marshall, still screaming, was hauled off her. Someone snatched her arm and yanked her up and out of the room, through the cabin and outside.

The two guards were peering into the cabin at the otherworldly shriek originating from within.

Tiana shook her head to clear it and steadied herself against Diving Eagle's warrior body. She touched the tender back of her skull with a wince. The skin around her neck burned and promised to bruise.

"What happened?" the Native demanded.

"My father's reach extends even here," she said hoarsely. She wiped away tears of pain and turned away from the cabin. "My father murdered Marshall's family. Every last person in the city who had a drop of Cruise blood in them was burnt. Marshall did not know, but I thought he should."

Diving Eagle released her, eyes pinned to her features as she spoke the difficult words. "Why would the Hanover do that?" he asked.

"Because he is mad," she replied. "Because he is the monster you believe him to be."

"You could have hurt Marshall. Ended his family line the moment he touched you."

"I am not my father," she said quietly, vehemently. "I have told you this many times. Arthur and I are different." She stepped away from him.

Diving Eagle was silent.

Tiana did not dare look up for fear of his judgment.

"You're a selfish coward, Tiana Hanover," he said finally. "You bear immeasurable power and think only to escape him when you alone may be able to stop him from destroying anyone else." Without another word, Diving Eagle strode into the cabin and slammed the door closed.

Marshall's scream was instantly quieted.

Tiana looked up, startled by the rebuke but more so

by the idea anyone thought *she* could do anything to oppose her father.

The image of throwing the skinwalker into the air returned to her thoughts.

What if he is right? She thought. What if she had spent her life feeling helpless and vulnerable and cowering away from anyone who spoke – but she and her hated deformities were strong enough to overcome her father?

She had not always understood her deformities and feared those monitoring her too much to test her limits. Whether she always had the level of ability needed to kill, or it was new, she could not know with certainty.

Was the Native right? Was she strong enough to protect herself now?

Rocky seemed to think so.

What is wrong with me? She thought, distressed. How could she possess an ability and fear using it to the point she cowered away from ... well, everything?

The faint presence of the skinwalker stirred at the edges of her mind. She turned to face the direction in which he was located. A new thought entered her mind. With a last glance towards the cabin, Tiana began to walk towards the forest.

CHAPTER SEVEN

THE STALLION BRED FOR ENDURANCE and speed lived up to its reputation. Twenty-eight hours after leaving the village, Arthur barreled through the city, past the smoky area where his father burned dissidents, and towards the pyramid at the far side. Cries from the Shield announcing the movement of a Hanover through the city followed him. He did not bother to stop and speak to any of the Shield members.

He had slept fitfully for a few hours atop the horse and was plagued by the same vision of his father watching the city fold in on itself and die. The images stuck in his mind, and Arthur had discarded the saddlebags and saddle – even his weapons – in order to relieve any excess weight so the horse could travel faster.

Half-crazed, praying his father had not had the

chance to act out yet, Arthur ignored everyone and everything, breezing past the soldiers who greeted him in surprise, the outer city residents who cried out in joy, even George, who appeared startled as Arthur galloped past him.

Arthur slid off the horse's back once he reached the stables behind the pyramid. A groom rushed out to take the horse, and Arthur patted the sweating animal before hurrying towards the entrance to find his father. From the corner of his eye, he saw George running after him and waving his arms to attract his attention.

Arthur ignored him. Nothing else mattered than ensuring his father was still present in the city and never left.

He reached the personal residences of the Hanover's at the top of the pyramid.

"Father!" Arthur shouted and strode past the guards stationed at the door leading into the apartments.

It was just past dawn, early enough in the day that his father should still be present in his quarters.

Arthur hurried down the hallway and stopped in front of his father's door. He pounded on the door.

"Father!"

Seconds later, a slave opened the door. Arthur pushed his way in, eyes wildly seeking his father's familiar form in the living area of the personal quarters of the Hanover ruler of Lost Vegas.

"Arthur," Edwin said and lowered his teacup. He sat near the window, reading the Shield's morning reports, appearing relaxed and rested.

Arthur bent over at the waist, sweating, dirty from the muddy path to the city, and panting.

"I did not believe I would ever see you again." Edwin rose and approached. He kept his distance with his hands clasped behind his back.

When he caught his breath, Arthur rose. "I negotiated my release with the promise of wealth," he reported.

"Your sister?"

"She is being held by our enemies," he said.

"And you return without her." The disapproval was clear on Edwin's face.

Arthur hesitated, uncertain how to respond. His father had rarely ever asked about Tiana let alone cared for her circumstances or even her health. Arthur had tried to convince himself the message he carried in his pocket – sent by his father to Chases Deer's father – was somehow misread, or perhaps, was an attempt for Edwin to manipulate someone into doing his bidding by using Tiana.

"You will have to return and negotiate her release. After you have rested." Edwin turned away and walked back to his chair. "And bathed."

While there was never affection in their relationship, Arthur was accustomed to some small display of warmth or at least, pride.

His father sat, picked up the report, and began to read again.

Arthur stood awkwardly after the dismissal. What had changed? Why was he, his father's heir, being rejected?

"I rode night and day until I reached the city," Arthur heard himself saying. "Are you not pleased to see me?"

"I will be pleased when you bring your sister home."

"You have hardly ever asked about her welfare at any point in my life," Arthur said. "I have been gone for weeks, Father."

"I did notice both your absences, if that is what concerns you," Edwin said with a glance.

Arthur waited.

When his father made no other response, a flicker of sadness settled deep inside him.

Is this how Tiana feels? The fleeting thought was replaced by another.

"Are you not interested in what I have been through?" he asked. "In the war brewing outside the city? The alliances among the Natives are shifting, and not in our favor."

"It would not be the first time in the history of our family that we faced such a situation," his father replied. "They know they have no chance to take the city. Do not concern yourself with such matters, Arthur. Your usefulness to me is your ability to bring back your sister."

Had Arthur heard his father right?

"The Cruises," Arthur tried a third subject. "Is it true what I heard? They are dead?"

"Traitors to the city and our family," his father said. "My own Cruise wife tried to murder my daughter, and did Marshall Cruise not try to murder you?"

"Yes, but –"

"Has your adventure outside the city made you soft? How can you forgive anyone who hurts our family?"

Arthur said nothing. His exhausted mind was filled with emotions and thoughts he had never considered before. The sense of having entered a parallel world, one that looked like his but was starkly different, returned. His father had always awed him in his calm handling of every situation he dealt with. Before this, never had Arthur considered the idea his father was incapable of feeling. He thought Edwin was a master at dealing with his emotions.

"You want me to bring back Tiana," Arthur said.

"Immediately."

"Father, I …" Arthur drifted off.

He had intended to warn his father about the vision. But his cold reception, and the experiences and insight he had collected outside the city, left his intuition whispering he should keep the vision to himself. For now.

"… I will go immediately when I am rested," Arthur finished.

"The sooner, the happier I will be with you."

"Very well."

Arthur turned away and left his father's quarters.

Deep in thought, he stood in the cul de sac where the bedrooms of all the family members were located.

He was accustomed to returning from the Winter Hunt to a parade and a feast, with his father speaking warm, glowing words about him in front of everyone in the outer city. Edwin Hanover had never been this cold towards his heir.

What did the newfound chill between them mean? How could his father claim Arthur's only use to him was to find the forgotten sister who only survived because Arthur ensured she did?

The vision of Tiana being chased by their father entered his mind again.

Whatever had changed with his father, it was potentially dangerous for more than Tiana.

"Sir?" George spoke and cleared his throat. "Your bath is being prepared, and food has already been delivered to your quarters."

Arthur blinked. How long had he been standing in the hall?

His eyes settled on his loyal slave, who had been the only person Arthur entrusted to check in on his sister for over ten years. Arthur motioned for his slave to follow him and entered his quarters. The scent of roast meat and vegetables and fresh bread struck him hard. Arthur's stomach roared to life. He had discarded his food the day before in his attempt to purge extra weight from the horse.

Arthur crossed to the table where another slave had just finished unloading a tray of food. He sat and began to eat, almost sighing at the flavors he had missed for several weeks. He wolfed down his food and waited for everyone but George to leave.

When his stomach was full, Arthur leaned back. "George," he started. "Something is wrong here."

George was quiet.

"Do you sense it as well?"

"I do," George confirmed. "Aside from your father ordering ten times the amount of people to be burnt each day, he all but declared you dead and Tiana his heir."

While not expecting this news, neither was Arthur completely caught off guard by it either. It explained the sudden change in his father's messages to Chases Deer. "Has he spoken to a clairvoyant?"

"I would not know, sir."

"From where does this change of policy – and heart – come?"

"No one knows. It was sudden. You missed his proclamation by no more than two days."

Arthur shook his head and stood. "I can explain nothing anymore," he said, mind racing. His father's rejection solidified resolve that had been building since he last spoke to Marshall. "I need for you to arrange a private meeting. In the inner city."

George raised an eyebrow. "You know no one approves when you visit the inner city."

"No one will know this time. I will take no Shield members with me," Arthur said. "Only you, I and this person are to know. Do I make myself clear?"

"Yes, sir."

Arthur provided the name Marshall had given him and only those details George would have to convey to convince the high-ranking member of the outer city to meet him. Once his slave had left, Arthur went to the bathroom for a much-needed bath and to think.

Several hours later, after resting, Arthur sneaked out of the pyramid in a slave's cloak with its hood up and walked through the outer city. Spring rendered the streets busier than they had been, and he passed through two small markets tailored to the pleasures of the upper class before crossing the bridge into the fish market and walking into the inner city.

The late afternoon was pleasantly warm, though mud still mired the streets. Arthur took a roundabout path to ensure no one followed him, his senses trained on the activity of the streets belonging to the poorer classes. Fatigue from his time outside the city lingered, and his tired mind and body wanted nothing more than to sleep until he was recovered.

But sleep was a temptation he dared not allow to lure him away from his visions. The political landscape had been dramatically altered by his father in the short time Arthur was away, to the point Arthur was not certain if he could trust anyone in the pyramid or outer city at all. Tiana had been tolerated but not valued by Edwin, and Arthur did not want to press the limits of where he stood with his father any more than necessary before he had some feel for all that had happened and what approach he could take.

He reached the rendezvous point – a market in a barn where illegal merchandise was bought and sold – and sank into the shadows to wait and watch for the man he sought. After an hour, he began to think either Marshall's ally was spooked after the mass burnings of the Hanover's political rivals, or that no one would trust any Hanover after all that had occurred.

His body grew stiff from the lack of movement, and he paced a few times around the small market. On his third trip through, he spotted the white hair and well-tailored cloak announcing the arrival of the man he sought.

As instructed, Gavin Ingram had left his personal guard outside. He stood out among the thieves and criminals in rags, and Arthur made a mental note not to meet somewhere quite so public, when his potential ally did not know how to dress to fit in.

Arthur tugged his hood down and approached the clueless Ingram.

"Follow me," he directed quietly.

Ingram jerked away.

Arthur led him out of the market and to a neighboring tavern populated by the same clientele as the market. No one looked up when they entered, and no one would ask questions.

Arthur sat on a bench at a table with enough room for Ingram to sit beside him.

Ingram did so. The wealth of his dress drew the attention of more than one criminal.

"You are not likely to leave here with your cloak and wallet," Arthur said with a half smile. He kept the hood to his cloak up. His father had mastered the art of finding those planning to kill him through a combination of visions, clairvoyants, and spies. Arthur would take the smallest risk possible, given he was sitting with one of his father's dissidents.

"This place is beyond unsavory," Ingram replied. "But I understand why you chose it. Your father would not think to put a spy here."

"You would know." Arthur lifted his hand to order food and drink in an attempt to fit in with the locals. "Does he still entrust you with the doings of his spies?"

Ingram waited until the server had left before

responding. "He has become very reclusive. More so than usual. But it is his prerogative, and I do not question the man who keeps our city safe."

Arthur chose to ignore the claim to loyalty. "I imagine he changed after my sister disappeared."

"Two days after," Ingram admitted in a low voice. "Also his prerogative. Why have you asked me to meet you here, Arthur? Why not in your father's council room, where we normally talk?"

"Do you have to ask?" Arthur asked with some amusement.

From the expression on Ingram's features, he was suspicious.

"We have a mutual friend," Arthur began carefully. "Marshall Cruise."

"Cruise?" Ingram echoed. "Traitors, all of them. Condemned to burn for their crimes against the Hanover family." The words were spoken in a rush.

"Marshall is alive," Arthur continued. "He is being held hostage by our former allies beyond the city. He is safe, if you are concerned."

Ingram wore the purposely-blank expression he always did when Arthur had seen Edwin address him during dinners and public events.

"He will not be safe for long, if my father discovers he is alive," Arthur added. "Marshall and I discussed the future of the city, and I understand your … group has big plans for it and for me."

Ingram glanced around.

"I know you intended to speak to me about this upon my return from the Hunt. Marshall confessed he was supposed to evaluate me and, if I were the person you all think I am, he would approve the decision for you to approach me," Arthur said.

Ingram was silent. Arthur assessed he was trying to decide if this were a trap or not.

"My father will destroy the city and everything around it for many miles," Arthur whispered. "I cannot stop him, if I do not have allies."

"How do you know this?" The question was careful enough that Arthur suspected more than Marshall knew the Hanover's were deformed.

"I have had a vision," Arthur said and drew a deep breath. "A very bad one. One that would unite me with your cause, even though I care for my father and my family's legacy. I cannot rule a city that does not exist, now can I?"

They fell into an uncomfortable quiet as the server brought each of them a plate of food. Ingram scowled at the dirty plate and fatty meat, but Arthur dug in.

"What exactly have you seen?" Ingram asked and poked at the undercooked root vegetables on his plate.

"It is as much what I have seen as what I know," Arthur explained. He quickly shared his insight into the brewing alliances among the Natives as well as the vision. He spoke of everything he had learned or foreseen – except for the visions about Tiana. Unable to explain his sister's presence in his vision, he had yet to decide how much to tell anyone about her deformities.

Ingram listened, his food ignored.

"I owe Marshall my life twice over," Arthur finished. "At first, I did not care to hear anything he said. But the more I saw of the world outside our city, and the longer I listened to Marshall, the deeper I understood the danger my father poses."

For a moment, the head of the underground opposition party sat in contemplative silence. He was too much the politician to reveal what he thought or felt in his expression, but Arthur guessed he was, in part, surprised.

"It is believed, among those few of us who have protected the knowledge of your family's capabilities, that your sister has inherited your father's unique traits," Ingram said at last. "And this is why he replaced you as heir."

"I have my own unique traits," Arthur replied.

"You do not display the level of deformity your father and his predecessors did."

"My father trained me, but always told me I would learn the true secrets to ruling only when I assumed his position."

"My theory is that he was waiting for your full abilities to manifest. They did not. But perhaps, Tiana's did."

It was Arthur's turn to be perplexed. "To what abilities do you refer?" he asked. "I have revealed my own deformities. They are not undeserving!"

"They are not," Ingram agreed quickly. "They will protect the city. But your father wields a different kind of deformity. The ability to move things with his mind, to *change* the composition of anything with a thought, to control the future he foresees, to replace the thoughts of others with his own. We do not know his limits, because he is very strategic in how he uses these gifts. He can alter the fabric of our universe itself."

Arthur could not recall ever witnessing his father use this kind of unnatural power at all. When he demonstrated to Arthur how to use his own abilities, Edwin had only used what power Arthur had. Arthur had no reason to believe his father possessed any other abilities than what he had displayed in private.

For the second time since returning home, Arthur had the sense he had never really known his father, or the depths of the secrets the Hanover leader maintained.

"Your father, and your forefathers, wielded absolute power, Arthur."

"And you think Tiana does now?" Arthur asked doubtfully.

"What you and I think is irrelevant. Your father appears to believe she is his heir."

Arthur wiped his mouth and dropped his fork, no longer hungry. "How did you plan to oppose my father? A man allegedly possessing absolute power?"

"We had intended to pit you against him by murdering your sister before her eighteenth birthday, while you were on the Hunt, and sending word to you that your father was responsible," Ingram admitted.

Arthur's mouth dropped open.

"Perhaps this is better."

"Better?" Arthur managed. "How so?"

"To replace one man possessing absolute power with another would condemn us to four more centuries of mad rule. You do not possess these deformities. You truly can become a different kind of leader," Ingram answered. "You might even save the city from this war you believe is coming."

Arthur's protective instinct stirred once more. Ingram did not address what he wished to do with Tiana, assuming she possessed these abilities.

"I must speak to the others," Ingram said. "How may I contact you?"

"Through my slave, George. I trust him with my life," Arthur said. "My father wishes me to return to the Natives soon to negotiate Tiana's release."

"I will contact you within the next two days. You

must not leave here before you hear from me, Arthur," Ingram said. "In the meantime, do as your father says. Keep his trust and if you are in danger, flee and send me word."

"Danger?" Arthur smiled. "Your concern is misplaced. He is my father. I do not fear him and his power."

"Have you never wondered why there are no cousins of Hanover blood, even though every leader bears two children at least?" Ingram asked.

Arthur's smile faded. He had cousins – but they were from his mother's and grandmother's kin, and not directly related to the Hanover's. He was about to reply that his family had a history of young deaths but abruptly realized that four centuries of siblings who died suddenly at young ages did not paint a very healthy picture of the intra-family politics of the Hanover's.

He had never thought to ask his father anything other about his uncle than his name and when and why he died. Edwin's brother had been poisoned, and Arthur assumed it was by the enemies of the Hanover's, and this was why his father was adamant about security.

What if the Hanover's had a much darker history to the deaths of family members?

Ingram rose. "Stay safe, Arthur," he said before walking away.

"Thanks," Arthur murmured.

He returned his focus to his food. Nibbling on

another piece of stringy meat, Arthur then pushed his plate away and finished his ale.

The meeting with Ingram had revealed more than he thought possible. Arthur's visions of Tiana's death had been accurate. Now that he knew the source of them, he could not help feeling uneasy about trusting Marshall's allies, even if they were the only people in the city willing to plot against his father. If they had planned to murder Tiana once, would they do it again, now that they suspected she was intended to replace the Hanover leader?

How could anyone – including his father – ever believe her capable of becoming the kind of Hanover who repressed and burned her people at the stake?

Or did the power corrupt every leader once it manifested? Would his sweet sister become like every other Hanover leader? Was this why she had crushed and flung the skinwalker five miles away?

No. Arthur would not allow this thought to take root. Tiana was not the typical Hanover – and neither was he. Everything he had done the past few weeks had been to protect her. If anything, possessing a deformity this great would allow her to learn to protect herself.

Maybe, she could help him depose their father and create balance and stability in a region that had never known either.

Maybe she can heal Warner, he thought. Whenever

he let himself think about his lover, his insides twisted, and his heart felt as if it were gripped in the vise of his chest.

He could not, would not, allow his despair over anyone's fate to prevent him from acting. His father had trained him since he could walk how to be an effective leader. The first rule was never to allow emotional entanglement to interfere with what needed to be done.

Arthur would find a way to save Warner. And Tiana. And Marshall. But he needed help, and he needed a mind clear of the fatigue weighing him down.

Arthur left the tavern and made his way through the city once more. By nightfall, he reached his quarters and locked the door then dragged furniture in front of the door in case Ingram was right, and Edwin Hanover planned on murdering his own son.

CHAPTER EIGHT

THE NEXT MORNING, AVELINE arrived to the city exhausted and anxious. Her first deep breath in the smoky city reeked of too many humans crammed into a small space – and it was the most comforting breath she had ever taken. She was tired of horses, of grass, of the forest. Lost Vegas was her home, and the moment she set foot in the city, tension released from between her shoulder blades.

As little as she cared for horses, or the bruises riding them left on her behind, she understood the usefulness of their speed and remained atop hers until she reached a familiar part of the city.

Aveline slid off the horse with a hiss and a groan in the ward known to house the Guild. She had been debating what to do for two long days during her journey back to the city. Long before fatigue fogged her mind, she had made the decision to go first to the Guild and reveal the fact she was alive, before pleading with her late father's former friends to help her find Karl.

Her time was short, and her plan to ambush Tiana's father relied on her conducting reconnaissance tonight. It was Sunday, and she had to know if Tiana was correct about her father being in the hidden passages. With no guarantees she could enter the privileged Hanover's apartments, she would need time to test the limits of what she could do before she began to explore the top floor of the pyramid to find other hidden entrances to the passageways where Tiana used to hide and spy on her family.

Aveline straightened and looked around. The horse would fetch money or provide her a means to leave the city and check on Tiana. After a debate about where she could fit an entire horse comfortably, she began walking through alleys towards the streets of the city's oldest market.

Aveline walked until she reached a quiet part of the inner city where one of Rocky's hiding places was located. The abandoned building served as a refuge for several criminals. She entered the shed behind it, whose door was marked in the lower corner by two crossed knives – the sign of the Guild – which Rocky had carved. While criminals were as likely to prey on other criminals as not, most were wise enough to leave assassins alone.

Entering, she saw that none of Rocky's clothing or sparse furniture had been disturbed. No one had bothered the discreetly marked hideout.

The shed was barely big enough for the horse. Aveline pulled off its saddle and bridle before maneuvering around it to leave the shed. She closed the door behind her. Her nose wrinkled at the combined scent of refuse and smoke.

The Hanover leader was burning more people than usual. The smoke rendered the grassland around the city cloudy and settled over the inner city in a thick fog. The sun was a glowing disk in the smoky sky.

Unsettled by the smoke, and by the thought of facing Tiana's insane father, Aveline left the shed at a jog with the intention of going to the Guild members and throwing herself on their mercy for help finding Karl.

If something went wrong this week, if Tiana's father used the deformities the Natives claimed he possessed to kill her, she wanted to die knowing she had found Karl or that the Guild would find him on her behalf.

Aveline's hands shook. She rubbed them on the leather material of her thighs, being careful not to rip her pants with the bear claw of her left hand. She wanted to write off her shakiness as exhaustion, but she could not take her mind off of what she had to do this night. She did not fear taking a life. She did not fear for her own life, either. But what caused her hands to shake and her heart to race? What filled her with urgency and wired energy when she had not slept in two days and was too tired to think straight?

Aveline self-consciously draped the edge of her cloak over her forearm and hand to hide it. She continued walking, only half aware of where her feet took her. When she realized where she was headed, she slowed.

She had intended to visit Guild Main and instead, was two wards away, near the home she had shared with her father.

Aveline glanced towards the sky and wondered if her father were watching her now and if so, what he thought about her case of distraught nerves on the week of her first official assassination.

She debated turning away from this direction and going to Guild Main. A thought stopped her, and she shook her head before continuing.

She wanted to visit her favorite place in the city one last time, before she spent the week researching how to murder Tiana's father. If she failed ... she would never be here again.

She continued through the fog until she reached the corner of the block where her father's house once stood.

The blackened shells of home and buildings met her gaze. Her breath caught, and she stared down the block where many of the high-ranking Guild members used to live or frequent.

The entire ward had been torched. She began to realize the dense smoke in the city did not just emanate from the burnings at its center, but rolled off of other parts of the city as well. It was difficult to see from outside the city, when all the smoke seemed to coalesce at the middle of the city and rose towards the sky in one thick column.

It's unnatural. Smoke doesn't move that way. The errant thought did nothing but muddy the scene before her. An area of the city known to harbor Guild members had been burnt to the ground. There was no way for her to know with certainty that the fire was created any other way than by hand.

Except ...

Aveline closed her eyes to focus her other senses on the destruction in front of her.

When Tiana used her magic, the air around her became charged to the point where Aveline was agitated by the strange energy. Tiana had charged the air around her without using her gifts in the Native village the night before Aveline left, leaving Aveline to conclude she was either growing more sensitive to the magic, or Tiana was becoming stronger.

Aveline felt that same charge in the city around her. Had it always been there? Was she just now feeling it, after her own unique deformity manifested?

Was this strange power the same causing the smoke to behave as it did?

Or … had it always behaved this way in the city, and she was just now noticing the world around her instead of dwelling in the comfort zone of the place she had always been?

She rubbed the fur on the back of her left hand absently, trying to make sense of the intensity of sensations running through her. She was more tired than she had ever been but felt compelled to run through the city or fight half an army. The charged energy racing through her blood would not abate enough to allow her to rest.

The city had changed since she left it a week prior, or perhaps, she had. She did not know with certainty which it was, but she understood the source of the urgency in her blood overruling her physical exhaustion. She had always been affected by the Hanover power.

Was she now feeling the power of Tiana's father? Was it possible for her to feel him when he was several miles away at the other side of the city?

Was he that strong?

Opening her eyes, Aveline could not decipher which frustrated her more: not knowing why she felt the way she did, or once more witnessing the aftermath of Hanover destruction. The Natives believed Tiana to be her father's heir, because of her demonstration of power in the center of their village.

What if they were right? And Tiana's power would one day rival her father's, to be felt throughout the entire city no matter where he was?

Would it drive Tiana mad, too?

It'll drive me mad if I don't stop it, Aveline thought, agitated.

She closed the distance between her and the remains of her home and stood in front of it. In her mind's eye, she pictured it the way it used to be, and her father alive within it.

She sighed, saddened by the memories and more so by the knowledge something very important had been kept from her.

"You could've warned me," she whispered to him. "You could have mentioned this." She lifted her deformed arm. "Or told me never to leave the city."

Was his spirit listening? Was he capable of regret?

If he were watching, he would want her to act like the daughter of the Devil. He would want her to respect her oaths, to fulfill all her duties with the discipline he had instilled in her. She had long since lost the envelope he left her that she swore to protect.

I messed up once. I don't want to disappoint him again. Leaving Tiana outside the city had not been ideal, but even her father could not find fault with assigning Rocky the protective duty for the Hanover girl. Rocky was her father's own protégée, the youngest assassin ever accepted into the Guild. Aveline had not abandoned her friend and was not about to turn away from the deal she made to save Tiana's life, and Jose's, from the Natives who held her.

Turning away, Aveline began walking towards the center of the city again. She broke into a trot then a run, needing to exert as much of the wired energy permeating the city and her body as possible.

She was out of breath by the time she reached the area where Guild Main should have been. Halting, she breathed in the smell of fire and burning wood, refuse and bodies. She lifted a hand to block the brilliant flames that had all but decimated the buildings crammed into this ward.

At the center of the fire was the hidden headquarters of the assassins. Dozens of people had gathered to watch the buildings burn. Few people spoke, and none of them wore Guild blacks.

Aveline hid her deformed arm and approached the crowd – then stopped abruptly. A new sensation smashed into the base of her skull, a strange pattering. For a moment, the pounding overwhelmed her. She took one step back then two, then turned and bolted down the street, until the beating at her brain was at a tolerable level.

Heartbeats. She had not noticed them in the Natives'

village, possibly because she was drugged up on pain medicines. She had encountered no one else on the path returning to the city, and she had avoided the crowds going to watch the public executions on her way to Rocky's hiding spot.

The crowd outside of Guild Main, her destination, erupted into heartbeats that slammed into her mind when she neared. She tested her ability to manage the discordant pattering at her brain. She could venture no nearer than ten feet to the gathered people without staggering from the pain of their heartbeats.

A week outside the city had ruined everything!

Hearing herself panting, Aveline scratched at the fur that covered her chest and neck. She retreated to the shadows of a nearby building while searching the crowd and passersby – whose heartbeats she heard before she saw them – for any familiar faces. She recognized many of the residents and frequent visitors to this part of the city without identifying any of the assassins who had worked with or for her father.

First the section of town where the former Guild leader and all his lieutenants lived and then Guild Main itself. The destruction of two strongholds of the assassin organization could not be coincidental.

Then again, she did not know the extent of damage done to the city by the mad Hanover leader. Judging by the smoke, more of the city was on fire as well. Were his attacks random?

What had changed in the city while she was gone?

Aveline glanced again towards the sky, this time to judge the time. It was early afternoon, shortly after midday. She would need days, if not weeks, to prepare for her assassination. She had only this night to determine if what Tiana said was correct about her father walking through the passages on Sunday nights. The Natives had given Aveline ten days. Two were spent in travel, and two Sundays fell within the timeframe they provided. If Aveline failed to reach the pyramid this night and conduct her reconnaissance, she would not know if she stood any chance at all at murdering the Hanover leader next Sunday.

Her eyes remained on Guild Main. If not for Karl, she would have journeyed to the Freelands with Tiana to ensure her friend made it then returned to the city.

She stalked away from the burning ward, mind racing between her two duties and the diminishing window of time she had to accomplish both. The throbbing collective of unharmonious pattering ease and stopped as she put distance between herself and the crowd. More heartbeats thrummed when she neared more gatherings and passed people. Individually, a person's heartbeat was tolerable. She experimented as she walked to determine how close she could come to others, and groups of people, without feeling as if her brain would explode.

How was she going to slip into the pyramid where Tiana's father and the social elite lived? How could she possibly survive her own deformity long enough to remain in the city for a week?

She wracked her brain to solve this problem as she sought out two more areas of the city where Guild members were known to hide out. Every area she went to was on fire or already embers, and she began to accept that the Guild's secret locations had not been accidentally destroyed, but targeted, which put her in a more difficult situation.

Their training, she knew from her father, would influence the assassins to scatter until the leadership determined it was safe to meet again.

She would not find a gathering of assassins, or the council that ran the underground organization, but what if she found *one* Guild member? Someone who could fill her in on what was going on and maybe provide insight into where Karl had gone?

After walking aimlessly for a few minutes, she found herself turning towards the center of the city. Her father's most loyal ally had always been Karl. Karl's brother, also an assassin, had lived close to the burn yard. Rocky had suggested finding Wilhelm. Aveline suspected he would be the last assassin to turn on Karl but could think of nowhere else to try.

Hoping not to find his home burnt to the ground,

Aveline treaded behind a small group people headed towards the center of the city. When their ranks swelled to a dozen, she fell back and touched her temple. Spotting the jammed streets ahead, Aveline broke away as close to her destination as she dared go. She made her way down a quiet street lined with brick buildings, each of which housed two hundred people or more. The pattering of heartbeats was quiet but present. She listened to the instinct that warned her a few seconds before the intensity of the sensations increased and slowed or quickened her step in order to avoid coming too close to anyone.

She had visited Karl many times when she was young and knew his brother to be located in the same building.

Alert and wary, Aveline entered the building and headed towards the fifth floor, where Karl had lived before he took up residency in the street where she grew up.

The beating at her brain grew louder, and she focused on sucking in deep, steadying breaths.

Open bays and private rooms alike lined the hallway. Aveline walked slowly through the dilapidated building and peered into rooms as she went. The bays were mainly empty. She sensed no more than five heartbeats in any one bay, with many of the individual rooms empty.

Passing a large bay, she paused to peer at the faces of the few men and women who had turned the open spaces into their homes before continuing on.

The sign of two crossed knives caught her attention, and she paused in front of a closed door leading to a private room. The small marking was faded and worn.

Aveline knocked.

No one answered.

A faint heartbeat came from within.

She counted to five then pulled a knife free and jammed it between the door and the lock. Aveline wriggled it until the doorjamb splintered. Keeping hold of the knife, she pushed the door open and eased in.

The ill-kept abode was well lit, though too cluttered for her to push the door open completely. Aveline squeezed into the living area and closed the door behind her. Was the state of the apartment a defensive mechanism? To trip anyone who tried to enter?

Her nose wrinkled as the scent of human waste reached her. Outside of the outer city, no one had indoor plumbing. Alleys were for dumping waste and refuse, but it smelled as if someone had missed the open window or not bothered trying.

"Wilhelm?" she called. "I know you're here."

Aveline searched the floor visibly for booby traps before taking several steps deeper into the quiet apartment. As she neared the single door in the apartment, from which the heartbeat came, she heard a strange sound. Part rattle, part exhale. Both sound and stench came from the room off the living area.

She gripped her knife and untangled her bear claw from the cloak, in case she had to fight.

With a deep breath, she entered the darker space of the bedroom and paused in the doorway.

Compared to the rest of the apartment, the bedroom was relatively orderly. Buckets of excrement and urine lined one wall, a bed the other, and piles of clothing and weapons were stacked neatly along the third.

Guild Blacks.

Her eyes went from the familiar clothing to the form on the bed. Pale, sweating and staring at her was a familiar pair of eyes. Wilhelm was younger than his brother by about fifteen years, but their features were similar enough for anger to light in her blood.

Karl's brother shifted onto his side as she stood in the doorway of his bedroom, but he did not reach for the weapons beside the bed. He rested an arm protectively over his abdomen.

He spoke first. "Are you here to take me to the spirit world?"

"No." Aveline lowered her weapons. Whatever was wrong with him, he was no threat. Feet from him, his heartbeat was faint and irregular, on its last leg, if she had to guess.

"I thought you were dead."

"Not yet."

"Shame. I'm ready to go." He eased himself onto his back once more with a groan.

"You are ill or injured?" she asked cautiously. She was not about to contract a terrible disease during the few days she had to plan the Hanover leader's assassination.

"Injured. Had a run in with the Shield several days ago. They left me for dead."

"You're not far from it," she assessed.

"Tell that to my spirit. It refuses to leave this crippled body!" His words came out with a rattle. He spat up blood, spit it into the nearest bucket, and then relaxed onto the bed once more.

"If you speak truthfully to me, I will fetch a healer," Aveline said and replaced her knife in its sheath.

"I am beyond a healer's ability to help," he said. "Can't you smell my leg from there?" He stretched to tug up one pants leg to reveal the black streaks originating from a deep slash that ran down his calf. The lower limb was consumed by gangrene and rotting.

"Remove the leg, and you might live," she said.

"Except for the blood in my lungs."

Aveline shifted her weight between her feet. Did she owe him anything? He was a member of the Guild.

But I'm not, she reminded herself. If his brother were present, he would tell her the same. She hardened. Tiana's softness was wearing off on her, if she were considering helping Karl's brother.

"I went to Guild Main to find your brother," she said.

"The Guild is gone."

"I know. I saw it burning."

"No, I mean, the Guild members are gone. We received the order to leave the city. The Hanover leader caught wind of an assassination plot and sent his Shield to track us all down and murder us," Wilhelm explained. "Hence my wounds."

"It was not the first time our people had been hired to assassinate them," she stated. "Why act now to take out the Guild?"

"Have you been in hiding?" Wilhelm's blue gaze settled on her.

"Assume I have," she said.

"The city has been in chaos for over a week. Water shortages, missing Hanover children, riots and mass burnings. It's been madness, with the Hanover leader at the center of it all," Wilhelm explained. "The Guild, every last member, was hired to ambush the Hanover leader and failed, and he retaliated."

"Who could afford to hire everyone?" she asked.

He shrugged. "It was handled by the leadership. What does it matter? We failed. Those who tried were burnt, murdered or disappeared. The rest of us were ordered to scatter once the Shield began hunting us. I can't move. I was assigned to get the message every Guild member passing through to leave the city."

"You remain loyal to the Guild?" she asked skeptically.

"Of course."

"Even after your brother left."

Wilhelm sighed.

"Why remain?"

"My brother and I are different people," he said curtly. "I owe the Guild my life, and so does he. He always resented your father for taking the leadership role. Karl was in line to become the leader, until the Devil's Massacre, after which your father brought in a benefactor who paid off the leadership council. He was voted in unanimously. Karl resented him for it."

"Karl was my father's friend. He helped raise me," Aveline said, unable to reconcile the man who helped raise her with the one Wilhelm described.

"Karl is complicated, but he never got over being passed up for the position," Wilhelm said. "I suspect the Hanover leader used Karl's knowledge to find us all."

"Karl betrayed everyone," she murmured.

"Or he was forced to reveal his secrets in the Hanover dungeon."

"He defected after my father's death and tried to turn me against the Guild," she retorted. "If this is his doing, he did it to curry favor with his new masters in the Trench!"

Wilhelm coughed again before answering. "Karl

petitioned the Guild leadership to make him the leader the night your father died. The Guild rejected him the next morning," he reported. "They promised him the position if he helped the Guild eliminate your father. Then they betrayed him."

Aveline went still. "Say that again."

"Your father was becoming a liability to the Guild. He became reclusive and secretive and controlling. He eliminated all the benefactors supporting the Guild, except for one, whose name he would not reveal. Everyone accepted his decision, until the money stopped flowing. Your father went into debt. The Guild did as well. It scared the other senior assassins."

She listened, not wanting to believe her father had been anything other than the strong, powerful leader of the criminal underworld she knew him to be.

"The Guild leaders went to Karl, who they thought knew who this secret benefactor was. They manipulated him for a second time." Anger entered Wilhelm's voice. "No one can forget the Devil's Massacre, and no one would oppose a man with your father's reputation. Poison was the method of choice, and Karl became your father's executioner."

Aveline had always thought her father's sudden death strange. He was healthy and strong. To die of a small cold? It had not made sense at the time, and now she understood why.

"Karl betrayed my father, then the Guild betrayed him," she said. "There is some justice in that." It did not help her feel any better. Acutely aware of the fur creeping up her arm, in response to her emotions, she struggled to contain the anger boiling deep within her. "Where is he now?"

"I've had much more pressing concerns," Wilhelm said and motioned to his leg. "I haven't seen my brother in weeks, since he walked out of Guild Main after they rejected him for the leadership position."

She half-heard his answer. Instead, Aveline was reviewing her interactions with Karl throughout her life, wondering if the answer had been in front of her all along. Had she been as naïve as Tiana to trust the man who seemed like an uncle? Had her father known Karl resented him enough to betray him completely one day?

How could anyone believe her father to be worthy of an assassination? The most celebrated assassin in the city's history? Surely he had an explanation for what he was doing!

Her harrowing experience after her father's death, when she was pursued by debt collectors and sold to a brothel, coupled with the skinwalker secret, left her doubting the father she used to worship.

"Why did the Guild lose faith in my father?" she demanded. "Everyone admired and respected him! If he made these decisions, he had a reason. Why didn't they just trust him?"

"You are naïve if you believe him above making a bad decision," Wilhelm replied.

Aveline's cheeks burned hot with embarrassment. Had she been blind to what her father was doing? Or had everyone else lost faith in a man who kept a secret he could not entrust with anyone else?

Raw pain trickled through her, last felt when she stood over her father's dead body.

Why had her father placed her life in danger? Why had he never shared the secrets of what she really was? Why had he lied about her mother's death? What was in the envelope he made her swear she would protect?

Why had he kept so much of the truth from her?

Had she ever really known her father at all?

There is a reason for all of this, a tiny instinct reassured her. There had to be. Perhaps there were topics he could not share with his daughter. Did he fear her judgment? Fear the truth would place her in more danger?

She blinked and noticed the tears in her eyes. Aveline wiped them away, not wanting to appear weak in front of Karl's brother, a full-fledged assassin.

"It's irrelevant at this point." Wilhelm coughed up more blood. "He's dead, the Guild is gone for now, and the Hanover leader is burning the city to the ground. All we need now is for the Natives to sweep through and murder every last one of us."

His words held more truth than he knew. Regaining her composure, Aveline flexed her bear claw. "You think Karl is involved with the Hanover leader."

"Or imprisoned."

She rolled her eyes. "Fine. Or imprisoned. Either way, you believe them to be connected."

"I do. The strikes on the Guild's members began a week ago. The Shield went from not knowing our identities to tracking and attacking us in a day's time. It's not coincidence."

"No," she agreed. "It's not." Her thoughts grew darker as she thought of Karl and the extent he went to in order to punish those people who had not wanted to promote him.

Then again, should she care about the Guild, when its members had participated in her father's murder? They had always been her extended family. She accompanied them to training and spent hours upon hours in her father's office at Guild Main. Many of the assassins played with her when she was younger, and many more gave her tips on how to fight and kill.

"Speaking of Natives ... what are you wearing?" Wilhelm studied her clothing quizzically.

Aveline did not respond.

"Take my blacks," he said and pointed to the clothing in the corner. "You won't be mistaken for a Native and burned."

Her eyes lingered on the clothing. Her whole life, she had dreamt of the day she would wear them, after a ceremony presided over by her father, and upon gaining the distinction of becoming the only official female assassin in the Guild.

After hearing Wilhelm's explanation behind her father's death, she found herself gutted at the thought of wearing the clothing belonging to those who betrayed her father.

Aveline glanced down at her Native clothing. "My mother was a Native," she said. "I'm not sure I know who my father was anymore."

A pattering of heartbeats sent pain ricocheting in her head.

Aveline left the bedroom to peer out the window.

Dozens of people were passing the building. She touched her temple. Spots appeared in front of her eyes. She left the window but could not escape what the presence of people did to her.

"Do you have pain medicines?" she asked.

Wilhelm snorted. "If I did, I would not be miserable and confined to my room."

"I have to go."

"Wait!" he cried as she turned to the door.

She did.

"Will you ease my passing?" he asked. "A favor from

one assassin to another?"

Aveline considered it. She held no warm regard for any member of Karl's family, and his death would not cost her a moment of thought. However, he was Karl's only living relative. If she did not find the traitor, she might need to speak to Wilhelm again or to use him somehow to lure Karl out of hiding.

"I'll return," she said. She then hurried through the trashed living area to the hallway.

More heartbeats smashed into her skull. She ran through the apartment building without seeing where exactly she went. Exiting into the street, Aveline sprinted away from the crowds, down an alley, and ran. She ran until the pain subsided, and she became aware of her mind once more.

She slowed and stopped, breathing hard. "Burn …me!" she cursed and gripped her head with one human hand, one bear claw.

What was the extent of her deformity? Why was it affecting her mind? She clenched and released her bear paw and stared at it. What did hearing heartbeats have to do with being a skinwalker, or half-skinwalker? Were the two talents connected?

Aveline stood in silence for a long moment. This time, her thoughts turned in a direction she had not wanted to think about.

Tiana, Diving Eagle, Rocky … even Jose … had

suggested she spent some time talking about her family past, and what she was, with the skinwalker Tiana had tried to kill. Aveline had shunned the Native side of her for her entire life, content to be her father's daughter without ever knowing anything about her mother.

But what if she needed to know something about her mother in order to survive what was happening to her?

She lowered her deformed arm and straightened with another look at the sky.

What did it matter who her mother was, when Aveline had no guarantee she would survive the week? The afternoon was creeping on.

Struggling with what she had learned, Aveline made the decision to focus first on this evening and verifying the Hanover leader's vulnerability. She would then have a week to gather the weapons and supplies she would need, find Karl and verify Wilhelm's account.

She began walking again towards the pyramid in the outer city. Assassins were trained to do one run through minimum to work out the details and account for obstacles or environmental factors which could not be planned for from a distance. If she did a dry run this night, and spent the week looking for Karl as well as finding out what she could about skinwalkers, perhaps she would be in a better position the following Sunday to execute Tiana's father.

Would the charged energy of the city allow her mind

and body to find enough peace to sleep?

Better add painkillers to my supply list, she thought.

Fur crept up her shoulder and across her chest. This question, above the others, caused her the most distress. Lost Vegas was her home, no matter how much of it was burning or who controlled the city. Would she have to drug herself for the rest of her life to stay in the city she loved?

CHAPTER NINE

TIANA FOLLOWED THE INSTINCT guiding her towards the skinwalker until nightfall. The early spring temperature dropped without the sun to warm the air, and she was soon shaking from cold. She hugged herself and continued onward, pausing occasionally to listen to the sounds of brush and branches rustling. The forest was as alive at night as it had been during the day. She lifted her eyes more than once to catch glimpses of the stars between pine needles. When she reached a small clearing, she stopped in the center and released a puff of air, watching it climb towards the stars.

The cold night was cloudless and moonless, a beautiful canvas of black sparkling with stars. She found herself fascinated by the combination of light and dark and how the two complemented each other. Neither stars nor sky overwhelmed the other; they lived in harmony.

The same could not be said for any part of her life.

I miss Arthur. And Aveline, she thought. The absence of her only two advocates in the world was acutely felt on a night like this. She tried not to imagine Aveline in her father's prison or being burnt at the stake, tried not to imagine Arthur falling back into line and overseeing the burning of any more families.

Two nights ago, she had experienced one vision of her brother in the city. Since then, no other visions of either of them had ventured into her mind, leaving her fearful for both. Chases Deer seemed to think Arthur was returning to confront their father, which placed him in more danger than Tiana was lost in the woods. And Aveline ... Tiana could not bear to think of what happened to her friend, if Aveline failed in her attempt to murder Edwin Hanover.

The only two people she cared about in the world were in the city, and she was out here, relatively safe in the forest.

Whenever she thought of her father, she wanted to cry or run or hide. She did not have the strength to oppose him. She was not Arthur, who was strong and fair and compassionate. She was not Diving Eagle, who seemed as if nothing could scare him, not even Ghouls.

Did Aveline and Arthur think she was a coward?

Aveline had been trying to toughen her up since they met. Arthur would never reveal his true feelings, but he hired Aveline to protect her.

If they did not believe her to be a coward, they at least both seemed to find her weak.

The worst part: she was weak in a way no one around her was – in her heart. How did she fix herself? Was it even possible?

The distant scream of a Ghoul interrupted her melancholy thoughts.

Tiana sighed and dropped her gaze to the forest. Ghouls were terrifying – but she had already faced them once and survived. Still, she had no desire to test her deformities again and began walking quickly in the direction of the skinwalker once more.

The sense at her mind told her his direction without offering any insight into the distance separating them. She grappled with this, uncertain how far she was willing to go to find him and prove to herself, if not the others, she was not a completely useless coward. Hungry and thirsty, she did not know how long her body would last her or what she planned to do when she found him or how to find food …

"Diving Eagle would not think of such things," she lectured herself in a whisper. "He would do what was necessary."

Resolute, Tiana glanced around without knowing

where she was exactly or how far the forest stretched. According to the map she made, north of Lost Vegas and past the forest, grasslands sprang up and filled the distance between the forest and mountains. She had never known exact distances, though, only recorded what she had overheard from others.

Did it matter?

She shook her head, tired of being conflicted and scared.

Tiana entered the forest and picked her way through the low branches and bushes, continuing towards the faint presence of the skinwalker.

Sometime later, long after she had lost track of where the meadow was, the flickering pulse of energy representing the skinwalker in her mind shifted.

Tiana blinked out of her thoughts and became aware of her surroundings once more. Shivering from the cold, she stopped to evaluate what had happened. Had she been too upset to pay attention to his movement? Why did he seem to be back the way she had come?

She looked around, perplexed. Without the sense of a Native or Arthur, who hunted in the forest, she had no way to know if anyone had been through here lately or if anyone was hidden in the trees or brush.

The Ghouls were active this night; their cries had remained distant but consistent, and she tilted her head. Were they tracking someone or were there a lot of the creatures in the forest this night?

Distracted by the cries that sounded closer than before, Tiana did not notice the tug at her energy, or the presence of anyone else, until a branch cracked beneath someone's foot behind her.

She started to turn.

A large hand snatched her by the back of her neck, holding her in place. Her deformities reared to life with her fear, prepared to strike out – only to be drained from her.

She froze, recognizing the sensation from her first meeting with the skinwalker.

The smooth, sharp edge of a curved blade slid around her neck. It pricked her skin, and pain fluttered through her.

… can't kill you but when I am done with you, you will wish I had …

Tiana swallowed hard at the skinwalker's thought. She wanted to cave in on herself, to cry and hope he acted quickly, whatever he chose to do to her.

But that was not how Arthur, Aveline, Diving Eagle, Rocky or anyone else she had ever met would react.

It was not how *she* could react if she were to confront her father one day.

Tiana forced back tears.

"I thought we had an understanding after our initial meeting," she whispered. "Whatever you do to me, I can do ten times greater to you."

"You read thoughts," his growl was low.

"At times. I know you cannot kill me. Is it because of what I am?"

The blade cut deeper.

Though her eyes watered, Tiana refused to cry or move away from the pain. She had spent the better part of her life in pain. There was only one truth about pain worth knowing: it always ended.

"Not always," the skinwalker replied to her thought.

… promise to your brother …

Tiana had never loved Arthur enough for all he did for her. Her heart swelled with affection for the man who placed himself in danger for her sake.

"We are at an impasse." Her voice trembled, and she cleared her throat. "You cannot kill me, but the moment you release me, I will make *you* wish you had."

"You do not wish me dead, spirit. Why have you followed me?" he replied.

The question was harder for her to explain than she planned. Did she tell him it was a matter of pride? Of proving herself to others? Of not feeling vulnerable anymore by facing someone strong enough to murder entire villages?

Or … was it because some part of her hoped he *could* kill her and spared everyone else the pain of tolerating her?

"Stupid girl," the skinwalker said.

She flushed, hating that he could read her mind and considered her as weak as the others did, even after experiencing her abilities firsthand.

"Alone, your advantage disappears. I know what … who … motivates you," the skinwalker added.

"Unfortunately for you, she is not alone."

Tiana's heart raced at the quiet, calm claim of Diving Eagle, from somewhere behind the skinwalker.

The silence grew tense, thick, and she held her breath, waiting to see what the skinwalker would do. Diving Eagle was no match for him, but the skinwalker was no match for *her.*

After a long pause, the skinwalker lowered the blade from her neck and released her. At once, her energy flooded back into her.

Tiana stepped away from the tall Native, whose tense frame and agitated magic gave her some indication he was close to snapping, even if he knew the danger in it.

Diving Eagle stood a short distance behind him, the muzzle of a handgun pressed to the skinwalker's head.

"I knew you were lying to me," Chases Deer stepped from the night, her weapon aimed at Diving Eagle. She uttered something to him in her tongue.

Diving Eagle retorted quietly without lowering his weapon or moving.

"You're fast, but you're not careful," Rocky responded

and appeared behind her, a knife at her back.

The cry of Ghouls was closer, and Tiana realized the creatures had been tracking the men and woman following her. Dismayed, she wondered if Diving Eagle had followed because he doubted her ability to do even this.

The skinwalker gave a low, smoky laugh.

Tiana was not certain what to do. The three Natives and Rocky were unmoving, each of them waiting for someone else to strike or back down, while none of them appeared willing to do either.

"The Ghouls are coming," she said.

"Two of us here will survive them," the skinwalker seconded. "One of us here cares if the rest of you live."

Were the words meant for her or the others? Tiana did not know, but she was not going to allow the obstinacy of the others to place them all in harm's way. She drew a deep breath and focused on all the weapons. Sweeping her hand upward, she snatched the weapons with her mind and sent them hovering into the air above their heads.

The skinwalker started away.

She blocked him, too. "You, stay," she said. "I found him for you." She addressed this to Diving Eagle. "But we must go now, before the Ghouls reach us. I cannot control my power enough to guarantee your safety, and the skinwalker will not defend you."

The Ghouls began to shriek. They had found their prey and were closing in. It was the instinct of a protector that made Tiana's blood fill with charged energy without her active summoning of her abilities. The colors of the world began to reverse as her body prepared itself for battle.

She grappled with the magic. She did not want Diving Eagle to see her lose control again, not when he already thought her a weak, selfish coward.

"I'm with you," Rocky said and approached. "Those two have some serious issues with each other." If he noticed Tiana's hair flying around, he said nothing.

"We are both survivors," Diving Eagle said.

"Agreed," Chases Deer's face was upturned towards the weapons. "I will deal with your lies later."

Assured the common threat deterred their tensions with one another, Tiana lowered the weapons without releasing her mental hold on the skinwalker. She focused instead on the power creeping through her body, preparing her. She knew without looking where the Ghouls were, and that the window of escape was already gone.

"This is your territory," Diving Eagle said to Chases Deer. "Take us somewhere safe."

No sooner had she tucked the weapon in its holster than Chases Deer moved into the forest, away from the sound of the hunting Ghouls. Diving Eagle motioned to

Tiana and Rocky.

"Too late," Tiana whispered.

The Ghouls, all ten in the hunting party, materialized out of the night and forest, glowing like specters. The first time she encountered them, Tiana had been too scared to notice their flowing robes or the gaping holes of their eyes. She had been controlled by emotion and adrenaline and reacted out of pure terror.

She felt the magic swell within her – but it didn't explode or overwhelm her as it had before with the Ghouls or skinwalker. She had not thought herself able to control it either of the two instances where it emerged from deep within her.

This was different. The colors of the world reversed, and Tiana remained aware. Seeing. Sensing. In control. She marveled at the sensations of being part of her body but also separate, as if the threats were not real, and she was in no real danger. Aware of the creatures staring her down, she felt Rocky tug on her arm.

"Go," she told him. "All of you."

"Aveline would murder me if I ..." he objected.

She faced him, and he fell silent. His weapons lowered, and an odd expression crossed his features. She did not have time to determine what exactly it was.

"Rocky!" Diving Eagle called from deeper in the forest. "Hanover!"

Rocky stepped back from her. "I'll let them know

you'll be along soon," he said.

Tiana returned her attention to the Ghouls awaiting her. She did not know exactly what to do with them or how to fend them off or even what she was capable of.

She heard whispers behind her but paid them no attention, instead trying to figure out what to do with the power whirling within her.

"Control," Diving Eagle called, his voice steady despite the danger. "Imagine them to be your father."

The words triggered her power in a way she did not expect. Tiana felt it roll outward, towards the Ghouls. It swallowed them. Several of them managed to shriek again before all of them, and every tree within fifty feet of them, exploded into tiny pieces, shooting straight up into the air and raining down not as flesh and blood, but as pine needles and pinecones. The needles and cones dropped into piles where the Ghouls and trees had stood.

The explosion was silent, as was the magic.

Tiana released her breath and gazed at the piles, puzzled as to how the creatures came to be plant particles. The colors of the world rippled into their natural hues once more. With the disappearance of the threat, her magic faded. Exhaustion, both emotional and physical, replaced the wired energy of magic in her blood.

"We know how she feels about her father," Rocky joked, though there was tension in her voice.

"We know more than that."

Tiana turned at Diving Eagle's cautious tone.

She had maintained control – and he had still found some part of her to be disappointed in.

She lowered her gaze and wilted before starting into the forest. "We should go."

The skinwalker was smiling coldly, the only person who seemed remotely pleased by the display. Chases Deer's mouth was open in shock.

Tiana hugged herself and walked without knowing where she went. She had taken a full twenty steps in a random direction when the others began to move again.

"This way," Chases Deer called.

Tiana altered her route without looking up. Rocky fell in beside her, while Diving Eagle trailed the woman warrior ahead of him. The skinwalker made up the middle of the procession.

Chases Deer moved swiftly through the forest, navigating unseen hurdles that tripped Tiana more than once. The cries of the Ghouls no longer followed them, and Tiana focused on not sprawling on the ground from the rocks, roots, branches and bushes in her path.

Soon, her lungs and thighs were burning from the effort of releasing her magic and navigating the forest all night, and she began to lag behind the Natives. Rocky took her hand and moved ahead of her, tugging her after him in an effort to keep their pace up.

The two Natives halted suddenly. The skinwalker

drew abreast of them. Tiana bent over to catch her breath before realizing Rocky had joined them. All four were standing over something, looking down in silence. Rocky squatted.

Tiana stood, embarrassed to be the only one out of breath – another of her weaknesses, if Diving Eagle were tracking them – and joined them.

When she saw what held their collective interest, she gasped and squeezed her eyes closed.

"He's an assassin," Rocky said. "Or was."

Do not be a coward, Tiana. Tiana ordered herself and forced her eyes open. Tears sprang into them, and she covered her mouth with a hand to quiet any sound of horror she might make.

The carcass of a man had been devoured from the waist up, leaving only a bloodied skeleton. His lower body appeared to be intact and was clad in black.

"What did this?" Tiana whispered hoarsely.

"Ghouls," Diving Eagle replied.

She swallowed hard and she began to wonder how she had been calm facing creatures that could do something like this.

"What was an assassin doing out here?" Rocky murmured and poked around at the clothing of the corpse's lower body.

"Meeting me," the skinwalker said.

"You?" Rocky echoed and peered up at the Native.

"For what purpose?"

The skinwalker looked directly at Tiana.

"When we are safe, we will talk," Diving Eagle said. "The corpse will draw more Ghouls and other animals. We need to go."

Chases Deer moved away, as did the skinwalker and Rocky.

Tiana remained, staring down at what remained of the man. "Should we not burn him?" she asked, her throat almost too tight to speak. "He is ... was a person."

"Any other time or place, yes," Rocky said. He returned to her side and tilted her chin up to meet his gaze. "Not tonight, Tiana." His look was warm.

She nodded and did not resist when he took her forearm and led her around the body.

Tiana let the tears flow down her face silently. She had only seen one dead body before – Matilda's. The image of what she had done to her stepmother was burnt into her mind. While she had not hurt the dead assassin, neither had she protected him from the Ghouls.

Weak. Coward. Broken. She could not stop thinking about how useless she was.

Soon, her attention shifted to keeping up with the others, and she channeled what energy she had left into running.

When Chases Deer finally stopped, it was at the edge of the forest, in what appeared to be an abandoned village, half of whose cabins showed signs of severe fire damage.

Tiana's eyes fell to the land beyond the village – and her heart stood still. Panting, she tugged away from Rocky and walked the twenty feet of remaining forest.

The grasslands glowed with stardust and rippled like water beneath the soft breeze. They stretched to the mountains whose purple blue shapes she had seen far in the distance, during the annual summer address her father made in front of the outer city.

The mountains were much closer, their towering forms creating a jagged skyline.

Mesmerized by the grasslands and mountains, as well as the knowledge the Freelands were somewhere beyond those very peaks, Tiana paid no attention to the others speaking but focused on the energy of the cold breeze sweeping over her. Aware of their positions relative to her, she was also aware of the skinwalker standing behind her a short distance.

"Why did you meet with the assassin?" she asked him.

"I do not share my doings with spirits."

"I am not a spirit," she said and faced him.

"You are not of this earth."

"Well, what are you?"

His sharply formed features cast savage shadows across his face. "A creature of this world."

Familiar anger and fear trickled through her. She

could not think of him without experiencing the vision that had driven her to attack him before.

But it had changed. Inexplicably so.

She started to turn away when she spotted the three who tracked her standing near a familiar cabin.

Tiana shivered. "We have been here before."

"I have not," the skinwalker replied.

"Yes, you have. Rather, you and I *will* be here. Right there." She pointed.

"You have foresight like your brother."

"What do you know of his deformity?"

"Deformity," the skinwalker repeated with a snort.

Tiana waited.

He said nothing more.

She studied him. Tall and lean, with one leg clad in black, the skinwalker's dark eyes were lifeless, his features incapable of warmth or compassion. She had seen shadows of his other forms and heard the Natives speak of his indiscriminate, mass slaughter, of his black magic.

And even he did not know what she was.

"Where is your friend?" the skinwalker asked. "The half-breed."

"Her name is Aveline," Tiana replied. "She was sent to the city."

"Has she changed fully?"

She shook her head. "Almost but no."

"If her body tries again, without my blood, it might

kill her, or she may be trapped as a beast."

"You murder everyone but you somehow manage to care about your wolf and her," Tiana stated. She touched the bracelet she wore, the one belonging to Aveline that matched the necklace the skinwalker wore. The mark was specific to the skinwalkers. "Because she is from your tribe?"

He rolled his eyes.

"I may not understand human nature much, but you saved her life when you did not have to," she asserted. "I know you care."

"She is one of my kind, and I am ... or was ... the last. My tribe was small. She is likely a cousin or niece. If I do not help her, she will die, and there will be no one left to follow my legacy."

"A legacy of murder?" Tiana regarded him skeptically. As soon as she said it, she had the feeling Aveline would approve of learning this about the family of her mother. Her protector had always intended to become an assassin. Perhaps both Aveline's father and mother were both assassins.

The skinwalker did not answer.

Her gaze slid to the faint ghost materializing beside him: a Native child with large eyes and a slashed chest. She had seen him in the vision, flanking the skinwalker.

"What was your vision?" the skinwalker asked.

"It was too short for me to know with certainty. But

we will be here, and you will ask me to help you."

"Your deformities could be useful, though I cannot imagine an opponent I cannot face on my own."

"I can," she said, thinking of her father.

"Someone you cannot defeat?" He appeared interested.

"I have never tried," she admitted.

"Coward," the child beside him whispered in an airy voice.

Tiana blushed.

"Ignore him. He is vengeful," the skinwalker said dismissively. "He knows the fears of those who can see him and leads them to their deaths."

Tiana shook her head. She knew nothing of spirits, let alone vengeful ones. That skinwalkers existed was enough to scare her.

"He's right." She released her breath.

"You nearly murdered me, a feat no one has managed in a hundred years. You should control those around you and rule them all. How can you fear anyone?"

"You, too," she muttered and crossed her arms. "My father is powerful and I ..." She trailed off without knowing how to finish.

"You are eighteen?"

Startled, Tiana glanced at the sky. If it was past midnight, then she was officially eighteen and had survived to her birthday. "Yes."

"Skinwalkers manifest their abilities around this age. You may as well. If you did not have the power to face him before, you do now."

"It is more complicated than that," she said.

"Because he knows better how to use his abilities."

"You assume he has them."

"You and your brother both do. They are passed down. I know nothing of your city, except the legend of the Hanover's, who have ruled un-challenged for four centuries," he replied.

It was harder to deny what everyone else assumed was true about him. Tiana wanted to think her father was not deformed. It was much harder to think he was – and lied to her and imprisoned her throughout her life because of her deformities.

"Do you sleep?"

She blinked at the odd question. "Of course."

The skinwalker smiled coldly. "I do not. Can you keep me here, and your companions safe, when your eyes are closed?"

Tiana had not thought about the measures required to imprison the skinwalker until Diving Eagle's father decided to use him.

"She will not have to," Diving Eagle said as he approached. "I know you have some respect for trade. I want to hire you, Black Wolf."

The skinwalker faced the newcomer and studied him

briefly. "You cannot afford me."

"You were eager to deal with me when I held the Hanover heir."

"And why did that negotiation fall through?" the skinwalker asked. "Because you attacked me in your village, perhaps? Or lost your prized possession."

"You had no intention of ever delivering on your promises," was the cold reply. "Your wolf stole our prized possession, and you would have slaughtered us, if not for the Hanover girl."

"That was the plan." Black Wolf smiled. "Saved by your enemy. I am certain you will repay her with a quick death."

Tiana listened to the exchange, wary of the skinwalker, in case he decided to attack either of them. When Diving Eagle did not immediately correct the creature, she shifted her focus to the Native.

"They will set me free," she said, prodding the Native.

"Will they?" the skinwalker challenged.

"Diving Eagle, your father said I would be free to leave."

His jaw ticked, and he looked at her finally. "That was not the original plan."

She stared at him.

The skinwalker chuckled.

Tiana was uncertain when – if ever – she had experienced the sense of betrayal sliding through her. It was not what she felt when she thought of her father.

This was different. Worse.

She had trusted someone, other than Arthur, for the second time in her life. Was her judgment as weak as her heart?

Was there no part of her free from deformity?

"I will leave you two to discuss your business," she said and started away.

"You do not need a master, spirit," the skinwalker said. "You can control them all."

Tiana ignored him. Part of her wanted to walk away without caring if the skinwalker slaughtered everyone once she was gone.

But another part of her – perhaps the deformed and weak pieces of her – could not bear the idea of anyone else being hurt. She left the immediate area but did not go too far to help, if the skinwalker acted out.

Cold and tired, Tiana sank down against a tree facing the grasslands. The soothing rustle of grass and pine needles comforted her some, though nothing could take away the pain she experienced knowing she had been betrayed.

Aveline and Rocky were both right not to trust the Natives who were eager to work with her. Like her father, they did not value her at all. No one cared for her, except for Arthur and Aveline, even though she cared what happened to others.

She wrapped her arms around her legs and rested her chin on her knees, shaking from cold but unwilling to be around anyone else at the moment.

Her eyes closed, and she began to doze, fatigued after the long night.

"You have to understand you are the enemy of my people," Diving Eagle said, interrupting her solitude sometime later.

She sighed, wishing she could be somewhere else at the moment.

He draped a cloak lined with fur over her shoulders.

"I am not like you. Any of you." Tiana tugged it around her, grateful for the warmth after her cold trek into the forest. "I do not care for a war I know nothing about, and I do not resent anyone or wish you ill."

"This is not the way of the rest of the world."

"I do not care," she said softly. "I have lived my life enslaved to others and wish only to be free of it all."

He was quiet.

"Have you been truthful with me about anything?" she ventured.

"Not about anything that mattered."

Tiana shook her head. "I suppose it is easy to lie to someone who does not know better, who trusts you at your word."

"It's not." His response was softer, without its normal edge. "We did not make this decision lightly."

"Perhaps it is my fate to be betrayed by those I trust."

"And you accept that?"

"That those who should protect me instead lie to me and plan to murder me?" she replied. "You are not the first. Why do you think I fear my father so much? I would not have seen this day if I stayed in the city."

"Perhaps you should place your faith in yourself rather than others."

She twisted to see him, frowning. "Why advise me at all? You plan to murder me." Anger fueled the words she would not otherwise dare speak to anyone.

"I said it was our original plan," he replied, meeting her gaze. "It was the council's preferred plan as well."

She waited, not quite grasping what he was saying and afraid to trust him, even if she assumed she knew.

"I cannot imagine any version of events where you live," Diving Eagle continued. "Your enemies … your father's enemies … will ensure you do not, and your innocence of how this world works, of how deeply this hatred of your family is buried in the breasts of men like me, will prevent you from knowing the danger until it is too late to stop it."

Coldness seeped deep into her, chilling her again, despite the heavy cloak. Aveline had tried to warn her of the danger of her inexperience.

"I cannot believe that men are so disillusioned by hate not to see what is in front of them," she said.

"And that is why you will die."

She felt the truth of this to her spirit. It was not in her to see the intentions of someone beyond their words or to believe everyone she met wanted her dead.

"My father has left the decision up to me," Diving Eagle said.

"I understand," she whispered, not because she did, but because the discussion was hurting her on levels she did not understand. It was worse than how she felt when he called her a coward.

She was ready to be alone with her thoughts, away from Diving Eagle's intent look.

"I do not wish you dead, Tiana."

It was the first time he had used her name. She frowned. "Are you lying to me again?" she asked.

"I will do everything in my power to ensure you live, unless your life conflicts with the lives of my people."

"Out of respect for your father?"

"Partially. If I am to become a great leader like he is, I need to understand the danger of allowing my pride to interfere with the truth. My father encouraged me to remain open when it came to you, to see the truth of who you are. I did not believe him at first." He paused.

Sensing there was more, she waited.

"His health has been failing for some time. I do not believe he will see the end of this war. Either that or ..." He frowned as he studied her. "... or you have triggered my gift. I am beginning to understand his words in a way I had not before." As he spoke, he rose and stretched his legs. "I will let you choose your fate, Tiana. I believe the skinwalker to be willing to work with us. You can leave, tonight, for the Freelands and never return. I will tell the council you died. Or, you can help my father and me lead a war against your father. I will not tolerate traveling with a coward. Those are your only choices."

Tiana's heart beat slow and hard against the cage of her chest. Before she knew how to respond, Diving Eagle began to walk away.

"Chases Deer is hunting for our next meal. Do not venture far," he said over his shoulder. "I will expect your decision by dawn."

She watched him, speechless, and then faced the grasslands again.

Diving Eagle was giving her a choice. Not only had she never expected him to offer her this, but the idea she alone could choose what happened next in her life left her feeling overwhelmed.

And ... conflicted.

How long had she dreamt of going to the Freelands? Her entire waking life!

But now? When her father could hurt her brother and Aveline any day, or the Natives could destroy the city?

Rocky dropped into a cross-legged sit on the ground beside her.

"I feel like I've missed everything my whole life," she voiced sadly. "I struggle to understand anyone, but Diving Eagle?" She shook her head. "How can he hate me so much? I do not even know him."

"He likes you."

"If this is true, I have misunderstood every interaction I have ever had with him!" she said.

"He is not an easy man to understand," Rocky agreed. "But he followed you out here of his own choice and put a weapon to the head of a skinwalker that could crush him faster than you would because he thought you were in danger."

"He followed me because he wanted the skinwalker to use against my father."

"Maybe." Rocky smiled.

He read people better than she ever would. Even so, she did not believe Diving Eagle was capable of liking her. If he decided not to kill her, it was likely because he no longer hated her. But the chasm between no longer hating someone and liking them seemed vast for a man who declared her to be his blood enemy.

Tiana doubted she would ever understand anyone.

"You look scared," Rocky observed. "What's on your mind?"

Everything. She thought. Nothing she could explain in a way that made sense. She felt no elation or excitement when she thought of the Freelands. While she wanted to go, the timing was off. Either she walked away from her brother and friend as war was about to ignite the region, or she stayed with no promise of surviving to see another opportunity to be free.

"Apparently he and the skinwalker came to an arrangement," Rocky added when she did not speak.

Tiana roused herself from her complicated thoughts. "They want him to murder my father, if Aveline fails."

"It's a suicide mission."

"What do you mean?"

"I mean, the Guild has tried to take out your father no less than a dozen times the past ten years. Aveline has the training, but your father somehow always knows. I don't know what he does to those assassins, but they're never seen again."

Tiana's pulse quickened. "You think she is in danger."

"I think anyone who challenges your father is in more danger than they can imagine."

"Then why did she go?" she asked anxiously.

"Because Diving Eagle threatened to kill you, me, and Jose if she didn't."

"I know but ... why did you let her go alone?" she asked, not caring about the emotion in her voice when Diving Eagle was not around to judge her for it. "Are you not her friend?"

"We were raised together. We may not share the same blood, but she is my little sister," Rocky said. A shadow crossed his features but was just as quickly gone. "I tried to talk to her about it but had the sense she already made up her mind. She would not risk your life for any reason, and not just because you are her sworn duty to protect, but because she cares for you. I believe she thinks that she can protect you if she eliminates the source of danger to you. While I did not agree with her decision, I understood and respected it. Aveline can handle herself."

Tiana could not think of Aveline and Arthur in danger without panic stirring inside her.

"And ... I'm taking the risk that you won't let her die in the city, and certainly not at the hands of your father," Rocky said.

"You think too highly of me," Tiana whispered.

"You saved her life and the lives of everyone in Diving Eagle's village."

By accident, and in such a poor fashion, Tiana was embarrassed an assassin knew anything about the incident.

"Ultimately, this is your life and your decision. You can leave any time you like," Rocky said more quietly. "Preferably with me. I tend to think you will be safer in the Freelands than anywhere around here and am happy to escort you there, if you so choose."

She searched his features before shaking her head. Her eyes found the skinwalker, who sat at the fire Chases Deer had started. "My whole life, I have wanted to be free. But not if it means I lose the only people I care about. That would make me no better than my father, who sacrifices entire families for his purposes. My deformities ..." she lifted her hands, and the branches of the tree above them pointed towards the sky. "... how can they be good? I am not strong like you. The thought of facing my father makes me want to weep! How will that help anyone?"

"Everyone fears something, Tiana. I don't understand the nature of your abilities, but I think, and Aveline agrees, that you don't have to become like your father. You can do good things with your deformities."

Then why was no Hanover leader in the city's history regarded as sane? Tiana did not feel madness when she used her deformities, but would she know if she did? How did she help others without also putting their lives in danger?

"I do not know what to do," she said.

"When you do, let me know."

She nodded. Her thoughts were heavy with new insight, and she could not help feeling Aveline, if not Arthur, was going to need her help soon and also that she was the last person in a thousand miles who should provide it.

CHAPTER TEN

AVELINE MADE HER WAY through back alleys, avoiding the center of the city, and crossed from the smelly, crowded inner city to the quieter, well kept outer city. Fewer people populated the outer city. Wealthy residents and their servants looked twice at her when she passed, though she waited until the last street before the pyramid to move out of the public street and into the narrower alley. Sweating from her quick pace, she rested briefly while watching the slaves and elite passing the mouth of the alley.

She listened to the heartbeats to identify any slave alone and moving at a pace that would make him or her easy prey. She had expected the charged energy to grow stronger when she approached the pyramid, but it remained steady. The Hanover magic was equally spread for miles. She did not recall sensing it outside the city, which meant either the city limited its affect, or the Hanover leader did.

Aveline identified one ideal slave by his heartbeat – until he crossed the mouth of the alley. The slave was close to seven feet tall and overweight. His clothing would never fit her well enough for her to look as if she belonged in the pyramid.

She retreated into the shadows of the alley once more and listened for another chance. As she did so, she could not help thinking the odd skinwalker abilities were going to be useful in her line of work. She could hear people, track them, without seeing them. She even knew what direction they were located, and how fast they were moving by their heartbeats. No dark room would ever challenge her again now that she was able to sense people no matter what the environment did.

A second candidate registered in her newfound ability. Aveline went to the edge of the street and spotted the woman ten or so years older than her and just her size. She left the alley and trailed, waiting until the unsuspecting slave entered an area with few other people.

Moments later, Aveline was walking down the street once more, this time clothed in the slave's robes belonging to the unconscious woman she left in an alley. A slave entering the pyramid was nothing to concern the Shield members posted around the large building.

The nearer she went to the pyramid, the more the pounding in her skull increased. Aveline lost precious time circling the pyramid to find the least busy slave entrance. If she could reach the top of the pyramid, which was sparsely populated, she would be able to tolerate the pattering of heartbeats in her mind.

Reaching that point, though, left her grinding her teeth.

It was dusk. By the time she went to the top of the pyramid, and found Tiana's passageways, it would be well past dark. She did not know how much time she would have to explore the hidden corridors and plot the right place to ambush Tiana's father next week. Feeling rushed again, Aveline recalled what her father had taught her about creating the perfect conditions for an assassination.

He would advise her to prepare and train and practice every detail of the mission.

I do not have time for that, she thought in frustration. She would have to walk in, assess everything from the layout of the corridors to hiding places, the responsiveness of the guards, the Hanover leader's schedule, ideal places to stash her weapons, an escape plan ...

The more she thought about all she had to do, the less hope she had at succeeding.

"One thing at a time," she told herself at last. She would now know how futile her efforts would be, until she determined the layout of the corridors and whether or not she would be able to hide within them. Every other part of her plan would hinge upon those passageways existing, being accessible, and Tiana's information being accurate. The most critical part of her plan was to survey the assassination location under the exact circumstances she would be in next Sunday, when it was time to execute the plan.

Aveline concentrated on using her ability to track heartbeats to find a way into the pyramid. She ignored the Shield members, who likewise paid no attention to a lowly slave.

The slave entrances were all busy. Disappointed, she chose the one nearest the private elevator leading to the top of the massive structure and braced herself to experience the pain of being around too many people. By the time she was ten feet in, her head was killing her. Aveline pushed herself onward. Rather than go straight up, she descended to the less traveled halls beneath the pyramid and stopped in a quiet hallway to breathe. The pounding lessened enough for her to refocus on where she was before she began to make her way through the hallways she had explored when bored.

She went to the laundry area and entered the steamy, hot bay where dozens of slaves labored over cleaning the clothing and linens of the elite. Wincing at the pain, Aveline took a more direct line to her destination than she would have normally. She pawed through several bins of dirty slave laundry before a flash of green caught her attention. Yanking the sash out that marked her as being a slave to the Hanover's, she exited the busy laundry room quickly.

After another break to ground her senses again, she ventured from the maze under the pyramid onto the main floor. The moment she set foot on the main floor, the hammering at her mind began. She staggered and leaned against the wall, waiting for a group of elite kids to pass. When they had, Aveline trailed them at a distance towards the servants' elevator.

She glanced towards the Hanover's private lift as she passed it.

The Hanover leader was exiting his elevator, escorted by three Shield guards. He headed towards the center of the pyramid.

My luck is turning, Aveline thought. She took note of the time and gauged she had an hour, maybe two, before he would venture into the corridors, if Tiana were correct about him being there around midnight.

The kids peeled off from ahead of her, also heading towards the center of the pyramid. Aveline all but ran towards the private elevator that would take her to the Hanover's private residences. She stepped in with another slave in green who eyed her before returning his attention to the linens he carried.

They left the ground floor, and Aveline breathed a sigh as the heartbeats of those people crowding the bottom of the pyramid faded. She sensed the two guards awaiting them long before the elevator stopped.

"You need help?" she asked the slave beside her.

"No, I –"

She grabbed half the stack of linens before he could finish. The slave glared at her. Aveline did not have the chance to assure him she was not trying to edge him out of his job before the doors opened.

The two guards outside the Hanover apartments regarded both of them closely before waving them past. Aveline released her breath, grateful they remembered her and that Tiana's father had not thought to put out an alert for the guardian of his daughter. He most likely assumed she would be with Tiana in the forest.

Aveline handed the linens back to the other slave, who grumbled a curse at her, before entering the utility room where extra linens and other service items were kept.

Aveline headed towards Tiana's old room, listening carefully for the heartbeat of anyone present. She heard no one and relaxed.

The door to Tiana's old room was nailed shut.

Aveline studied it then her bear claw and rested it on the door. Her deformed hand was much larger than her normal one, and she hoped, stronger. She used the long nails to slide between the door and the frame, drew a deep breath, and wrenched the door open.

Nails popped out of place and landed with the tinkling sounds of metal on marble behind her.

Impressed by her own hand's strength, Aveline collected the nails before she opened the door and entered Tiana's quiet room.

It was even smaller than she recalled. She gazed around in distaste, remembering the weeks she spent there as well as the incident with Tiana and Matilda. The room had been scrubbed clean of even the smallest sign of blood from the incident. With the window boarded up again, it was dark, and Aveline turned on the light to the bathroom.

She went to the closet and opened the door.

Frowning, she looked over the wall where the entrance to the passageways had been. Wood boards over fresh concrete blocked off the passageway, and Aveline debated what to do. The passage had run around the cul de sac of the apartments, to Matilda's former room and Arthur's. She had explored its length once and did not recall any other entrance into the crawlspace.

Aveline touched the new wall. Breaking through it, or attempting to, could very well take a week and tools she had no idea how to sneak up to the Hanover's apartments. The sound of destroying the wall alone would guarantee her discovery or capture.

A heartbeat reached her.

She left the closet and turned off the light, listening and waiting as it approached. It paused in the hallway outside the door before continuing into what she judged to be Tiana's new room.

Aveline peeked out into the hall and saw Tiana's door open. Satisfied it was a slave and not a guard, she closed the door and waited for the person to leave. A few minutes later, the person exited and retreated down the corridor leading to the personal quarters of the Hanover's.

After another moment of debate, Aveline left Tiana's old room and stood in the center of the hall. She had never been in Arthur's room or in the Hanover leader's quarters. Tiana's passageways had run from her closet to Arthur's room on one side and Matilda's on the other. She said she heard her father move around beyond the corridor. Given the layout, it was logical to assume, if there were a second entrance into the hidden passage, it would be through the Hanover leader's quarters.

Aveline went to his door and tried the knob. She was not surprised to find it locked. Unlike Tiana's door, she would need a gentler approach than prying this one open with her bear claw. She pulled the lock pick kit, which had been part of the fancy weapons Arthur gave her. Within seconds, she had the door unlocked and pushed the door open.

Aveline stepped into the Hanover leader's quarters,

tense and ready to confront anyone lingering inside, even knowing no one was. She did not know what to expect of his quarters, but it was not to find the immaculate rooms to be normal. The décor was masculine and far more subdued than Matilda's gilded chambers had been. The windows were opened, and the room smelled of a combination or roses and citrus cleaner.

Uncomfortable knowing whose room it was, Aveline gave it a cursory search before going to the wall where she suspected a passageway entrance would be. The Hanover leader's quarters were smaller than Matilda's with three separate rooms off the main living area and two bathrooms. The apartment floors were all padded with expensive rugs and the walls bedecked with drapes and antiquated paintings Aveline guessed were from the Old World.

In order for Tiana to hear someone on the other side of the wall, she would have had to have been parallel to Arthur's room, which put the passageway at the end of the apartment away from the bedroom.

Unlike the other rooms, there was no window to provide light in the small area. Aveline turned on a light in the hallway and pushed the door open fully. She entered. The room had been turned into a museum or treasure room by the walls packed with paintings, domed glass over jewels and ancient books, and other trinkets and objects cluttering every inch of surface space available.

Ignoring everything, she concentrated on the wall neighboring Arthur's quarters. She went to use two hands to explore, but her bear paw was too large to do what the fingertips on her other hand could. She traced the space between paintings with her fingers, searching for any sign of a hidden passageway: cracks in the wall, breezes where there should not be any, or anything else to give away the entrance.

Close to the corner of the wall this room shared with Arthur's quarters, her fingers slid between two paintings – and kept going. She pushed farther, waiting to meet the wall but did not feel it.

Aveline wiggled her fingers to determine how much room she had then carefully slid her bear claws into the space.

"Don't fall," she told the paintings on either side. She wrapped her fingers and claws around the door behind the art displays and pulled.

It did not give. She shifted her hips to give her more leverage and tried again.

The door leading to the hidden corridor slid open to reveal darkness.

Thrilled to know Tiana was right, Aveline stepped through the entrance. A faint pattering against her skull reached her the moment she did. She pulled the door closed behind her, wary of being discovered by a slave.

Confident the Hanover leader would not be returning until later, she stood still, waiting to see if any light source would become apparent.

None was, and she stretched her hands out straight in front of her, walking forward until she found the wall of the passage. She turned left, away from the direction where Tiana's hidden corridor lay, and began to move slowly down the hall. Her hands trailed on either side of the passage. Without knowing what kind of flooring was installed, or if there were obstacles, she placed her feet carefully, one directly in front of the other.

She counted twenty feet before her toe hit something solid on its way down. Aveline used her foot to feel around before settling it on a stair. The heartbeat was becoming stronger, not fainter, and she paused on the bottom stair to read the senses she was not comfortable with yet. It was possible someone was in the Hanover leader's room, whose wall she walked inside. But it felt like the heartbeat came from ahead of her, not the side or behind.

It was not Tiana's father ahead of her; this much she knew. She did not fear meeting anyone else and planned on leaving before she stumbled upon a slave or anyone else.

Her pulse quickened, and she drew a knife, just in case she needed to threaten a slave. She took another step, then another and another. The stairwell was the same width of the passage – narrow enough for fingers to touch both walls when she held out her hands – and spiraled as it led her upward, into the steeple of the pyramid.

Someone was definitely ahead of her. Aveline continued, her senses listening for any sound the person had begun retreating down the stairs towards her. The devil's blood inside her stirred with its eagerness for confrontation, and fur crept across her body.

The heartbeat remained where it was. Aveline crept forward, pausing at intervals to ensure the person had not moved, and she had time to escape if someone did.

The spiraling stairwell was dark and silent, aside from the brush of her boots against stone, until the curling of its ascent stopped. Light – candle or torchlight by its warmth – edged a door at the top of a straightaway directly ahead.

It was then she noticed the second heartbeat. It came from behind her – and was closing fast. She had been too focused on her destination, and the person ahead, to pay attention to what followed. The heartbeat that trailed her was strong and steady, and it struck her that the heart ahead of her seemed ... weak, fluttering in comparison. Arrhythmic. It had not moved at all since she first sensed it.

Whoever was ahead of her was not ... normal. She had not noticed the difference until she contrasted it with the normal heartbeat of the person climbing the stairwell behind her.

A shiver worked its way down her spine.

Uncertainty fluttered through her. She had not thought about *why* the passages exited or why Tiana's father sneaked away from his guards and family weekly to enter them.

Who – or what – was secreted away at the top of the pyramid?

The unnerving sense of her bicep expanding in response to her emotions reminded her how important it was for her to remain in control. Aveline stretched and steadied her breathing, aware of the progress of whoever followed her. His heart remained slow, his step unhurried, as if he did not yet know she was present.

She searched the area around her before realizing that she faced only two options: straight ahead or back the way she came.

Aveline began to climb again on her tiptoes. With luck, the door ahead of her hid an apartment much like the others with multiple rooms. She would have a chance to hide before the person following discovered her.

What about whatever is ahead of me? She gripped her knife harder, unable to make sense of the unusual heartbeat awaiting her.

By the time she reached the door, every inch of the skin on her neck was engulfed with fur, and it had spread down her chest to her stomach. With another deep breath, Aveline opened the door a crack and peered through it.

Only one room appeared visible. A fire burned in a hearth opposite the door, and she smelled herbs. No one was present in her restricted view.

She pushed the door open more fully, eyes roving the area and knife ready to strike. This room was well lived in and consisted of two chairs, a small table, rugs, the hearth, and two wardrobes. A second room, which had been beyond her initial ability to see, branched off of the small space. Sweat popped out on her forehead and body. The air was heavy and hot, similar to the laundry rooms beneath the pyramid. But it was not just this that left her skin crawling and her devil's blood agitated.

Charged energy. She felt like she was standing beside Tiana the day the Hanover girl killed Matilda. The sensation was thick enough, Aveline found herself shaking out her arms, as if she could push off the energy bombarding her.

The heartbeat behind her grew nearer.

Aveline closed the door behind her and looked for a place to hide.

Someone stirred from the other room. The heartbeat remained faint, fluttering, its rhythm unlike anyone else's she had heard.

Did it belong to an animal? If so, why had she not

noticed her horse's heartbeat? Or the hearts of the rats infesting the inner city? She could think of no other explanation for what it was, or what else the Hanover leader hid in the attic of the pyramid.

After meeting the mad, if enigmatic Hanover leader, she did not think he would be hiding an animal up here. Whatever it was, he hid it here for a purpose.

Aveline inched forward rather than retreating to hide in a wardrobe, agitated by the energy and perplexed by what her newly awakened senses were picking up.

She reached the doorway of the second room and froze. Her mouth dropped open. How long she stood there, she did not know, until someone spoke from behind her.

"Little assassin. We meet again," Tiana's father said.

Before she could react to the words, Tiana's father had touched her. Lightly. On her arm.

Hot energy shot through her, stirring and feeding her devil's blood. Aveline staggered and dropped to her knees. Pain and power roiled and swelled within her. It was stronger than her, fed by Tiana's father – and familiar.

As she writhed on the floor, Aveline recalled when she had first experienced it, the day she arrived to the Native's village. The day she could not remember.

"Why is my daughter's protector here without her?" the Hanover leader mused. He stood above her, relaxed, with his arms folded across his chest. "You are both eighteen this night. Congratulations. You made it."

Aveline fought to control the instinct to transform, triggered by the Hanover magic. She convulsed, bewildered by the sensitive senses of an animal that were overtaking hers.

"I cannot have you talking about what you found." Tiana's father said with a glance into the room. "But I cannot kill you, either." He leaned down and touched Aveline again. "It is said killing a skinwalker brings years of bad luck upon someone." His amused smile chilled her to her core. His charged energy shot straight through her again. Her devil's blood roared to life, destroying her attempts to control it.

"Find my daughter. Return her to me," he ordered quietly. "Quickly."

Aveline's clothing ripped. Fur raced across her body, while her muscles bulged and expanded to several times their normal sizes. The necklace bit into her neck without snapping. The transformation was agony. Her body tore itself apart slowly only to begin rebuilding seconds later. Her scream turned into a roar, and her hot tears dripped down the long muzzle that replaced her nose.

She screamed until her throat was raw.

The Hanover leader's words pummeled her brain, searing themselves into her mind. The compulsion to obey was as strong as the instinct to attack him. For several moments, as she transformed, the conflicting urges warred within her – his will against hers. Finally, her body ceased bucking and changing and went still. The image of Tiana was forefront in her mind, and the desire to fight fell away.

Aveline hauled herself to her feet. Her animal senses and human senses clashed, rendered her surroundings a blur of color, smells and sounds she could not fully make out.

"Go. Now," Tiana's father commanded her.

A whisper crossed her mind, a memory, a reason why she should resist.

It was swallowed up by animal instinct and the compulsion to obey, fueled by the Hanover magic corrupting her devil's blood. Aveline turned and barreled away, out of the room, and into the dark stairwell.

"Run, assassin!" the Hanover leader shouted after her.

CHAPTER ELEVEN

THE NIGHT BEFORE, ARTHUR'S dreams had consisted of the vision of his father destroying the city. Over and over, until he could feel the ground beneath his feet tremble each time the city collapsed.

Unable to face another night of visions, he prowled the city streets as he and Warner used to do when bored. The weight of the city's impending doom was made heavier by the knowledge he had been all but ordered by his father to leave in the morning.

In a few hours, when dawn broke, Arthur was expected to be sitting atop the horse he road into the city, ready to obey his father's command, and find his sister.

But if he left ... there would be no city to return to. His visions left him no doubt as to the fate of everything around him.

If he stayed, he would have to defy his father.

No one who ever openly opposed his father had survived the day.

Ingram had not contacted him again, and his hope of finding support in Marshall's allies had faded with the sunset this day.

Dressed in black, and wearing a mask, Arthur crouched on top of a building to peer at the damage done to part of the city by his father. No one could explain what his father was doing, or why he set parts of certain buildings on fire and not the entire ward. His father's council had rebuffed Arthur's attempts at conversation. It was not entirely because of Arthur assuming Tiana's position as the rejected Hanover child.

It was fear. He had seen it in their eyes. The meetings and gatherings inside the pyramid held the same dead air surrounding the burnt, collapsed buildings of the city. No one would so much as whisper insight into what his father was doing or planning.

I cannot leave the city until I am certain it is safe, Arthur thought again and rose. As his father's original heir, he had the importance of preserving the city drilled into him from a young age. His father had burnt many a person in his time leading the city, but he had never attacked the city itself.

What made him turn on it? The mercurial Hanover

leader was becoming the largest threat facing the city four hundred years of predecessors had strived to protect.

Arthur could not ignore what his visions were telling him. His father would decimate everything.

Arthur paced restlessly before nimbly scaling down the building to stand in the quiet street whose lampposts had been likewise destroyed.

How did he stop Edwin without allies among the powerful? It was not as simple as facing one man – but one man whose deformities granted him an unknown amount of unnatural power in addition to all the people who would back him out of fear.

"How does one man save a city?" Arthur whispered to the ashes he faced. He could not ever recall being helpless. His whole life, he had been the Hanover heir and commanded respect, power and loyalty by virtue of his birth.

Alone, he began to understand the enormity of a task leading the city truly was. It took a different kind of power than being born in the right household. It took courage and compassion and allies. His father, mad as he was, deserved admiration for managing and protecting a city that would have perished long ago, even if his draconian measures lacked consideration for the life of his people.

Did his father's lack of compassion make it easier to lead? If he were not concerned about preserving life but the city as a whole, no matter how many people had to die?

Arthur did not know the right answer, just as he struggled to find any solution to curtailing the danger the city faced.

Over and over, he drew the same conclusion. He could not leave. The visions were too strong, lingering long after they should have, for him to dare leave his father alone with the city.

But what difference would it make if Arthur remained and could not stop his father?

Tired of arguing with himself over the impossible problem, Arthur turned away from the destruction and started towards the other side of the city and his home. The only good he saw in his situation was that his lover, sister and Marshall were safe outside the city. If he could not stop his father, or ended up imprisoned or dead, those he cared about would have a better chance of surviving on their own among Natives that resented them than facing Edwin Hanover and his strange power.

The rest of Lost Vegas would suffer, though.

Arthur sighed.

By the time he reached his home, it was close to midnight. He removed his mask before emerging from the shadows of the street leading to the great pyramid and tucked it in a pocket. The Shield members greeted him quietly, but none of the elite residents of the outer city would look him in the eye when he passed them. Before Arthur headed towards the elevator that would take him to his apartment, his faithful slave, George, moved to intercept him.

"Sir, there is a matter requiring your attention," George said brusquely.

"From the friend I had you visit yesterday?"

George nodded.

"What does he say?" Arthur asked eagerly.

George hesitated. "Will you follow me, sir?" he asked.

Arthur nodded.

The slave led him out of the pyramid and into the night. He paused in the shadows of a stack of crates containing food that were being unloaded from several carts.

The normally unflappable slave lifted a black piece of cloth, his cheeks red. "Forgive me, sir. I did not want to agree, but they insisted."

"Paranoid, are they not?" Arthur took the hood with a smile, hoping to reassure his slave. "I will do what I must," he said and slid it over his head. "Lead on, George."

"Wait here."

Arthur obeyed. George left his side. Moments later, a horse nuzzled Arthur's arm. He touched its face briefly before someone spoke.

"Mount, please," Ingram directed quietly.

Arthur obeyed.

Ingram took his reins and led him away from the pyramid. The sounds of movement gradually disappeared. Arthur listened and timed their travels. They made two turns, crossed the paths of few people, and generally rode straight away from the pyramid. He was able to identify the moment they left the city by the change in the sounds of the horses' hooves on the ground. The city bore cobblestone and dirt streets; the roads leading out of Lost Vegas were a mix of stone, gravel and dirt.

When he assessed they were safe, he addressed the conspirator. "I expected to hear from you sooner," Arthur said.

"We had to verify parts of your story," Ingram replied. "We are cautious."

"As well you should be," he agreed. "Should I take this journey outside the city as a sign you have decided in my favor? Or are we headed to my execution?"

After a pause, Ingram spoke again, this time from beside Arthur instead of in front. "Your account of what occurs beyond our city appears to be truthful. We are unable to verify whether or not Marshall lives, but our leader has chosen to act after the events of the past week."

"Leader. Are you not the third most powerful man in Lost Vegas?" Arthur mused. "Who would a man like you answer to?"

Ingram did not answer.

"When will I meet your co-conspirators?" Arthur prodded.

"You will meet one now." An amused note was in Ingram's voice. "Though I doubt you will thank me for it."

Arthur did not know how to take the statement. "I am supposed to leave tomorrow morning. Has your leader taken this into account?" he asked. "I cannot oppose my father's command."

"We are aware. Through our other channels, we learned your father intends to send four of his personal Shield guards with you tomorrow morning. They have one order, and it is not to escort you to the forest."

Arthur understood the possibility of his father turning on him, but the words still fell like blows. He shifted atop the horse, struggling with his emotions. From cherished heir to ignored nobody, he had plummeted in worth in his father's eyes in a matter of days. Knowing his father's cruelty, should he experience the sense of loss yawning open at his core? Should he yearn for his father's acceptance?

"I am sorry, Tiana," he murmured under his breath. He had never understood her pain in being rejected, or why she always asked him about their father each time they spoke. He shook his head. "I do not intend to die tomorrow."

"We agree. But we think your father needs to believe you are dead, in order for you to help us," Ingram said.

"Ride out as planned tomorrow morning. There is but one route towards the north. We will arrange for your group to come under attack by Native allies before the Shield members can execute their orders. You will be dead in name, with your father's guards as witnesses."

Arthur listened.

"You will then secretly return to the city afterwards and work with us to overthrow your father."

While effective, it was not the greatest plan Arthur had ever heard. His instincts bespoke of no danger from Ingram and blared with danger whenever he thought of his father. Ingram, and his co-conspirators, had everything to fear from the failure of their plan, including the loss of their families. They were taking a risk in trusting Arthur, let alone saving him.

Arthur's vision played through his mind. "I have no choice," he said. "The city is doomed. I cannot leave it in the hands of my father. Of this, I am certain. My visions kept me awake all night."

"The same you shared with me?"

"Yes. Absolute destruction."

"What of your sister?"

"What of her?" Arthur kept his tone neutral.

"Have you seen her in this vision?"

"No."

Ingram was quiet again. He slowed his horse and then stopped both of their mounts. "Your sister is believed to be cooperating with the Natives. Are you aware of this?"

Arthur shook his head but was not surprised by the news. He could not imagine what the Natives wanted from Tiana, unless she was as powerful as Ingram seemed to think she was. In that case, everyone could find a use for her, and she was too naïve to know her own danger.

Not for the first time, he silently thanked Aveline for being present to help his sister.

Ingram's original plan – to pit father and son against one another in the hopes Arthur won – returned to Arthur's thoughts. Was there a chance Tiana was the key, since she was believed to have inherited his father's much speculated about powers? Was that why Arthur's initial visions had been of his sister in danger? Why his father was chasing Tiana through a field in the latest version? Why the Natives wanted her help?

He did not trust Ingram enough yet to voice his thoughts.

Ingram dismounted. "Come down," he told Arthur.

Arthur obeyed and waited. He heard the nickering of other horses and assessed they were no longer alone.

Ingram removed the hood, and Arthur blinked to focus in the night. Ingram stepped aside to reveal a man whose features were familiar but whose face was not. Half a dozen other men, wearing all black to include hoods to hide their faces, stood behind horses behind the stranger. Arthur studied the man, uncertain why he felt he should know him. His hair was the same shade of blond-red as Arthur's, his blue eyes as well. He was older, in his fifties, seasoned by the sun with leathery skin, tall and sporting a fighter's build.

Ingram had brought Arthur outside the city and behind a nearby hill. They were invisible from the road and city yet close enough for the Native scouts watching the city to remain at a distance.

"Arthur, I would like you to meet Simon Hanover," Ingram said quietly.

"Hanover," Arthur repeated. He studied the stranger, suddenly understanding why he appeared familiar. Simon bore the same features as Arthur – and Edwin. "Uncle Simon Hanover who died from poisoning shortly after I was born?"

"That was the rumor," Simon replied. "As a general rule, a Hanover will not kill another Hanover. But we will hire someone else to do it for us. Every once in a while, an assassin fails. Or is paid off."

Arthur was speechless, disbelieving.

"We do not have much time," Simon said and closed the distance between them. He motioned Ingram to step back, and spoke in a low voice for Arthur alone to hear. "It seems the Cruises were right. I spent years tracking a skinwalker to kidnap you, and all I had to do was ask for a meeting." His smile was fleeting. "I wanted to look you in the eye so I knew you were serious about betraying your father."

Arthur shifted. "You hired the skinwalker," he said, recalling Black Wolf's claim.

"I did. I ordered an assassination on your sister as well."

"And you are plotting to murder my father." Arthur did not know what to think. A man who should not exist was leading a silent rebellion against his father.

"I am. Do you agree to help us?"

Arthur heard the dangerous note in his uncle's voice, the one that told him Simon Hanover was not beyond murdering his own kin. "My goal is to save the city," he replied slowly. "Whatever form that takes, I will support. But it is my city, and I will not let it suffer any longer. If you intend to replace my father, then I will not hesitate to dispose of you as well."

Simon held his gaze. The two stared each other down, while Ingram shifted away, lest they resorted to violence.

"Arthur," Simon said. "I do not want the city. I want to stop the madness that runs in our family. I have heard from many people you will make a strong leader."

"Then why did you bring me here? Why not approach me in the city?"

"Because I cannot enter the city. Your father's power prevents me."

"He knows you are alive?"

"Initially, he believed me to be dead. I survived on my

own, outside the city, for several years, before he figured out I was alive. I made friends of the Natives and have been hiding among them. A failed assassination attempt alerted my brother. I have not been able to move as freely since then."

Arthur glanced at Ingram. "What do you want, if not the city itself?"

"I told you."

Arthur raised his eyebrows. "No one goes to this extent, and risks the lives of so many people, to walk away benevolently when it is over. There must be a reward in it for you."

"Spoken like a true Hanover," Simon said with a smile that did not reach his eyes. "We will discuss more later. For now, we will work together towards our common goal."

Arthur recognized deception when he saw it. "What of my sister?" he asked quietly. "What is your plan for her?"

"That will depend upon your sister and the actions she takes. If she behaves like a Hanover, she will be treated like a Hanover."

Although Tiana had never once behaved like a true Hanover, Arthur could not stop the churning in his stomach. The man before him was as dangerous as Edwin.

"Do you share my father's abilities?" he ventured.

"I do not. I share yours, or deformities similar to

yours in their extent," Simon answered. "We are the lesser sons, the Hanover's that do not normally survive."

Arthur sensed this was the truth.

"Go. Before your father notices your absence, or Ingram's." His uncle moved away towards the horse awaiting him. "You do not trust me, Arthur, and I do not blame you. You will tomorrow morning, after you see how we work. The Natives will help us stage your death."

Or they will kill me, Arthur added silently.

No part of him trusted his uncle completely. What choice did he have? This plan was the only one that might allow him to live long enough to save the city and reunite with Tiana. For now, it would have to be enough that he shared a goal with Simon, and that Simon hated his brother enough to try to depose him.

Arthur would take the political high road and play along, until Simon showed his true hand.

Unsettled by all he had learned, suspecting his sister was in great danger from Simon and Edwin, Arthur mounted his horse and rode with Ingram back to the city. His thoughts reeling and instincts fluttering between alarm and acceptance, he said nothing to his companion as they sneaked along secondary streets towards the pyramid.

"Is Marshall really safe with the Natives?" Ingram asked when they reached the stables.

"Are the Natives not your allies?" Arthur retorted.

"They are your uncle's allies. I have little experience dealing with them. Marshall risked his life to sway you. I would like to know not all the Cruises have been sacrificed."

Whenever Arthur thought of Marshall, he was torn between guilt and regret. Marshall had lost everything in his pursuit of Arthur, and Arthur had nothing to offer in return but the reality of what his father had done to the Cruises. Why had Arthur not listened to him sooner? How had he ever chosen to ignore the horrors his father unleashed upon everyone in the city?

"He is safe. The Natives are awaiting the ransom I promised for him," Arthur confirmed. "Whose plan was it to murder my sister?"

Ingram was quiet for a moment. "Simon's."

"And whose was it to try to recruit me?"

"Marshall's."

Arthur felt sick to his stomach. Marshall's compassion, and devotion to non-violent politics, ran deeper than Arthur had ever suspected.

Nothing I can ever do will make things right for him, he thought.

"We are finishing the planning for tomorrow and will send word in the morning before you leave," Ingram said.

Arthur nodded. Distraught, certain he could not sleep after tonight's revelations, he turned away from his home with the intention of roaming the city again.

A scream froze him in place. It came from inside the pyramid and pierced the night to float for blocks in each direction. An involuntary shiver ran through Arthur. He turned around to gaze up at the pyramid.

It was not a human scream. Neither was it an animal's roar.

It was something in between – and familiar.

Skinwalker. His instincts answered before he could search them for what it was. He and Marshall both had heard that horrible sound on more than one occasion when they were trailing the skinwalker through the forest.

"Find shelter," he said to Ingram and bolted towards the pyramid.

Confused members of the elite were milling in the entrances and ground floor. The Shield had yet to react – and why would they? Arthur alone understood the danger and source of the sound.

He paused when he reached the cavernous interior and let his senses adjust to the noise ricocheting off the walls. The scream bounced around him, until the inner pyramid was filled with a deafening roar. With some effort, and the assistance of his deformities, he determined its source: the apartment at the very top.

Unable to explain how a skinwalker could possibly be in his home, Arthur nonetheless sprinted to the elevator reserved exclusively for the Hanover's and rode it with great impatience to the top.

Before he reached the family's private residences, the sound suddenly stopped.

He sprang out of the lift as soon as the doors opened, past the baffled guards, and down the hallway.

Arthur drew his weapons, already knowing they were useless against the creature he had seen destroy villages, and slowed his pace.

"Father?" he called.

"Sir, the Shield –" one of the guards shouted after him. The man trailed him towards the other end of the apartment.

"Go." Arthur turned and snatched his tunic. He hauled the guard close. "Keep everyone away! Do you understand?"

The guard nodded hastily and stepped back. Arthur waited for him to leave the hallway before focusing again on what was before him.

With any luck, the skinwalker would not be willing to murder him, until he had fulfilled his end of their deal.

Questions poured through Arthur's mind as he moved towards the faint flicker in his mind indicating where the creature was. How had Black Wolf made it this far without being seen? How had he accessed the most secure residence in the building?

How had he done anything without leaving a telltale path of slaughter behind him?

Arthur drew a deep breath to steady himself as he tiptoed down the hallway. His father was present in his quarters, though Arthur's magic was unable to tell what condition his father was in. He was torn between two conflicting thoughts: hoping the threat to the city was dead and praying his father was alive. Anger fluttered through him.

Arthur pushed his feelings aside to focus on his current objective.

Oddly enough, his magic indicated that the skinwalker was in Matilda's room, which Tiana had told him transitioned to her after Matilda's death. Arthur passed his room and his father's then paused in front of Tiana's.

He opened the door and entered, bracing himself for an attack.

"I know you are here," he whispered to the dark room beyond the door. Easing the door closed, he breathed deeply, took a step, and then stopped to listen.

A growl resounded from deep within Tiana's quarters.

"We have a deal, friend," Arthur reminded the skinwalker.

Was it capable of comprehending a person when in its beast forms? Arthur had not thought to ask this or any of the other questions suddenly entering its mind.

He took another step.

The growl grew louder.

He stopped.

"Do you remember me?" he asked. "Remember our common friend? The sweet creature who protects you? Who helps me?"

The growl subsided without disappearing.

"You do know who I am," he said.

His mind told him where the creature was. The fact the skinwalker wasn't attacking was the best sign Arthur could imagine.

"I am placing my weapons down," he said. "Then we can talk." He lowered his knives, heart pounding loudly in his ears. "See? They are down." He pushed them towards the skinwalker with a foot. "You are in no danger." He dropped his hands to his sides.

The growling stopped.

Arthur licked his lips anxiously. Either the beast was preparing to pounce or was calming down. "Come on out of there," he said and stepped closer to the closet in which the beast hid.

Silence filled the room. Outside the door, he heard the clatter of Shield guards gathering.

Arthur retreated and locked the door before returning to his place near the closet door.

"Those men outside the door will overreact when they see you," he warned the skinwalker. "While I'm well aware you can take care of yourself and murder everyone for miles around, I also know this floor can be locked down completely. You will not be able to escape the building, no matter how many Shield members you kill. You will have no choice but to leap out the window. Even you cannot survive that fall, my friend." He inched closer. His stomach turned over and over, and his instincts – reading the intentions of the creature – were torn between warning him away and telling him it was safe. "I can help you. Come out, and we will leave here together."

Arthur held his breath. The stillness of the creature was as telling as its growl. He waited despite knowing how likely it was for the Shield to break down the door soon. He was no longer the heir to his father, but he was still his father's son and one of the only two Hanover's currently located in the city.

Come on, he urged the creature mentally.

The beast stepped one foot out of the closet without making a sound. Its fur was the color of night, its eyes glowing the shade of the moon.

Arthur noted the eye color but did not have the chance to dwell on why it had changed from the last time he saw the beast.

The skinwalker took another step out of the closet then a third and fourth. It stood, the hair on the back of its neck standing on end, and its body crouched as if to attack. It had not chosen the form of a bear this time but of a great black panther.

"I have not seen you in this form before," Arthur said.

"You seem ..." *smaller.*

The words died in his throat. Moonlight from Tiana's windows reflected off a medallion around the beast's neck, and the reason behind the noticeable changes in the beast suddenly made sense to Arthur. During the time they shared together in the Diné village, Tiana had shown him her medallion and explained how her guardian possessed an identical one that lit up when they were close.

Arthur's eyes widened, and he stared at it ... at *her* ... in quiet disbelief.

"Aveline," he breathed finally. To some part of him, buried deep enough it was intertwined with his instincts, he was expecting this. The daughter of the Devil had always been special in the same way Tiana was: in her blood. Arthur knew from the moment she appeared in a vision to him, even before he sent out search parties to find the elusive assassin-in-training who was destined to become his sister's guardian. "What are you doing here?"

The skinwalker's mouth opened, and she made a quiet, plaintive sound. Arthur tilted his head, hoping to hear her words, as he often did with Black Wolf's spirit guide. No words or images formed in his mind.

"Can you not turn human? I will understand you better," he said.

She shook her head.

"You cannot turn human?" he prodded.

Another shake.

Before Arthur could respond, one of the Shield members pounded on the door.

"Go back in there and hide," he ordered her quietly. "We can sort all this out later. I need to protect you first."

Aveline obeyed and slinked back into the closet.

Arthur went to the door and yanked it open. "Whatever it is, it is not present here," he told the phalanx of Shield members jammed into the hallways. "Has anyone checked on my father?"

"We evacuated him," one of them reported. "We will do the same for you."

"Gentlemen, I am one of you," he said and smiled. "Who better to show you the hiding places no one other than my family knows?" He walked into the hall and closed the door behind him. "No one is to enter the sacred personal space of Tiana, the Hanover heir, unless he is accompanied by my father or me."

No one objected to his firm tone, and Arthur pointed to his father's quarters with one hand and his with another. "Search those two rooms and report to me your findings."

Five Shield men piled into each room, and another two into the cramped space of the room where Tiana once resided.

Arthur remained close to the door to Tiana's quarters. As if suspecting the danger her movement or sound could place her, Aveline did not stir from within the dark space.

Arthur managed to subdue the flurry of thoughts running through him. His situation had become more complicated than before. If Aveline were unable to turn into a human, and Arthur had an appointment to fake his own death in the morning, how was he supposed to sneak a panther out of the pyramid beneath dozens of watchful Shield eyes?

ABOUT THE AUTHOR

I breathe stories. I dream them. If it were possible, I'd eat them, too. (I'm pretty sure they'd taste like cotton candy.) I can't escape them - they're everywhere! Which is why I write! I was born to bring the crazy worlds and people in my mind to life, and I love sharing them with as many people as I can.

I'm also the bestselling, award winning, internationally acclaimed author of over sixty titles and counting. I write speculative fiction in multiple subgenres of romance and fantasy, contemporary fiction, books for both teens and adults, and just about anything else I feel like writing. If I can imagine it, I can write it!

I live in the desert of southern Arizona with a pack of spoiled dogs and Tubbs, the Godfather cat who rules them all.

CONNECT WITH LIZZY

Website: LizzyFord.com
Facebook: www.Facebook.com/LizzyFordBooks
Twitter @LizzyFord2010

Radish app: LizzyFord
Instagram: @LizzyFordAuthor

ALSO BY LIZZY FORD

Non-Series – 2014 - 2017

Black Moon Draw (about a reader sucked into her book)
White Tree Sound (2017- sequel to Black Moon Draw)
Highlander Enchanted
The Door

History Interrupted – Time Travel Romantic Adventures
West
East
North (2017)
South (2018)

Lost Vegas Series – young adult post-apocalyptic
Aveline
Tiana
Arthur
Black Wolf

Spell Realm Series – young adult fantasy
Water Spell (2017)
Dragon Spell (2018)
Moon Spell (2018)
Sword Spell (2019)

Super Villainess Chronicles
It's Not Easy Being Evil
It's Not Easy Being Good

Omega Series
Omega
Theta

Alpha (2017)

Omega Beginnings Miniseries – individual episodes
ALESSANDRA
MISMATCH
PHOIBE
LANTOS
THEODOSIA
NIKO
Cleon
Herakles
Omega Beginnings Miniseries – complete set

Trial Series
Trial by Moon
Trial by Thrall
Trial by Blood
Trial by Heart

Theta Beginnings Miniseries
Silent Queen
Shadow Titan
People's Champion
Supreme Magistrate

Starwalkers Serials (with Julia Crane) – new adult
science fiction serial
Severed
Trapped
Exiled
Revealed
Escaped
Ascended

Heart of Fire – sexy dragon shifter
Charred Heart
Charred Tears
Charred Hope

Incubatti – Buffy meets 50 Shades
Zoey Rogue
Zoey Avenger

Rhyn Trilogy – new adult paranormal with demons
Katie's Hellion
Katie's Hope
Rhyn's Redemption

Rhyn Eternal – Death finds love
Gabriel's Hope
Deidre's Death
Darkyn's Mate
The Underworld
Twisted Fate

War of Gods – paranormal with gods, guardians and
exceptional humans
Damian's Oracle
Damian's Assassin
Damian's Immortal
The Grey God

Damian Eternal
Xander's Chance
The Black God

Hidden Evil – paranormal with angels and four horsemen
Hear No
See No (2017)

Speak No (2017)

Unnamed Series
Unnatural (TBD)

Anshan Saga – new adult science fiction romance
Kiera's Moon
Kiera's Sun

Santa's Ninja Elves (short stories)
Natasha & Hunter

Non-series titles – 2011 - 2013
Star Kissed
A Demon's Desire
The Warlord's Secret
Maddy's Oasis
Rebel Heart

Witchlings – young adult paranormal
Dark Summer
Autumn Storm
Winter Fire
Spring Rain

Broken Beauty Novellas – new adult dramatic fiction
Broken Beauty
Broken World
Broken Chains

Voodoo Nights - young adult paranormal
Cursed

Writing as SE Reign, erotica writer
101 Nights Box Set (featuring all seven serials)